SHADES

A BRACKARD'S POINT NOVELLA

GEOFF COOPER
BRIAN KEENE

POLTERGEIST PRESS

POLTERGEIST PRESS

ISBN: 978-1-913138-24-0

www.poltergeistpress.com

For Norman Partridge, with respect and admiration.

Acknowledgements

Geoff Cooper:
Thanks to my friends, those that have stuck by me through both the thick and thin. I could have made it without you, but I'm glad I didn't have to.

Brian Keene:
Thanks to Cassandra and Sam; Jim Moore; and my readers.

The authors would also like to thank Alan Clark, Richard Chizmar, Mindy Jarusek, Brian and Kate Freeman, and Kelly Laymon.

Authors' Note

THE FOLLOWING STORY, set in the Eighties, takes place in the town of Brackard's Point—the fictional setting for most of Geoff Cooper's stories. The town is located in Rockland County, New York, on the west bank of the Hudson River, under the shadow of Hook Mountain. Prior knowledge of the Brackard's Point mythos is not required for you to enjoy this novella. All are welcome. However, if you are a long-time Coop reader, then you'll see some familiar faces, albeit at a different stage in life than when you first met them.

This story also features elements from Brian Keene's "Labyrinth" mythos. The Labyrinth is a dimensional shortcut between worlds, universes, and realities, and is only accessible to those who know how to open the doors. Again, prior knowledge of the mythos is not required or necessary for you to enjoy this novella. All are welcome. However, long-time Keene readers will spot some familiar pathways.

We hope that you enjoy *Shades*. Thank you for your patience and support.

Geoff Cooper and Brian Keene

SHADES

ONE

To Danny, the choice between sitting in school and making money was no choice at all. He would be twelve in a month. He'd been in the school system long enough to know that you made shit sitting in a stupid classroom. The yuppie kids from Snowdrop could ask their parents for whatever they wanted—and get it. They had allowances and trust funds. But kids from The Hill had no such benefactors. Kids like Danny—and his friends, Chuck, Ronnie, Matt, and Jeremy—had to figure out their own way to get stuff. Their parents were no help. Between the rent, groceries, and paying off bill collectors, none of their parents had money for frivolous things like their kids' desires. If they *did,* they would live somewhere else.

Everyone who lived on The Hill dreamed of living somewhere else.

Danny's hope of leaving The Hill died when he was seven. That year, shortly after Labor

Day, his dad's body was found slumped over the wheel of Mr. Amiratti's black Cadillac. Suddenly, Danny's life was shot to shit because some Italian douchebag didn't want to pay respects to some other Italian douchebag and the crazy sons of bitches started blasting each other. And when Amiratti's Irish driver got in the way? Well...that was too fucking bad.

Story of Danny's life, so far. *Too fucking bad...*

Amiratti lived. Danny's father wasn't so lucky.

After his old man's death, Danny's mom started drinking. The Giordano family, who owned the Happy Bottle Shop liquor store, drove a Lincoln. Their kids had new clothes for school and new video game systems the day they went on sale. They had allowance money. The Giordanos took vacations together, returning after the Christmas break with January suntans. His mom helped pay for all this, while he got shit.

Danny had never been further than twenty miles from home. He always wished to go somewhere else. Leave Brackard's Point and go...away. Anywhere was good, as long as it wasn't here. That dirt bike he wanted might get him somewhere. It might not, either, but at least he'd have *one* of the things his father had promised him: *a dirt bike, season tickets for the Yankees, fancy restaurant food all the time...*

Danny didn't mind working for his money—especially on nice days. It was better than being broke. He kept the money stashed away in his secret hiding place under the carpet in his closet. He used to keep it between the mattress and the box spring, but moved the cash after his Mom found it. She would have spent it all on booze, so he took the envelope and ran. Later, when she confronted him, he told her that it was a dirty magazine and suffered a grounding he didn't deserve. Not that it mattered. She soon forgot about his punishment anyway. She did that a lot—forgot things—except where the money was hidden. His mom had a nose for it. Sometimes, she took money from his jeans, and left little I.O.U.s scrawled on scraps of paper that she had no intention of repaying and forgot about the next day. But Danny never forgot. His rusty, piece of shit Schwinn five-speed served as a constant reminder.

He'd rescued the bike from a junk pile and fixed it up with some help from Matt, Chuck, Ronnie, and Jeremy. Once they got the thing road-worthy, Danny was proud of the bike. He loved the freedom of mobility that it offered. But the glory had long since faded. Now, the bike was just an embarrassment. Ronnie and Jeremy made fun of it. He needed something better—that YZ-125 dirt bike. If he got it, that would shut them up, once and for all. Shut everyone up—even those rich snobs from

Snowdrop. And even if they *didn't* shut up, even if he was wrong, all he would have to do was gun the engine to drown them out.

That was his dream. That was why he'd cut school on this gorgeous spring day, and what had brought him to the water.

The Hudson was brackish this far south; the air smelled of salt and fish and sewage. Blue crabs lived in rocky crannies along the shore. During low tide, Danny sometimes walked out onto the flats between Brackard's Point and Haverstraw. He'd snatch the crabs from their normally concealed hiding places on the exposed rocky reefs. Luis and Maria, who ran the Haverstraw Marina Bait Shop, always paid him cash for a five-gallon painter's bucket full. They touted them as *FRESH BAIT! LOCALLY CAUGHT!* As if that made a difference—no one in their right mind would dare eat anything that swam in the Hudson. At least, he hoped not. Sometimes, he worried about making someone sick by selling Luis and Maria the crabs, but most of the time he could put such thoughts aside.

The lure of the dirt bike was stronger than his conscience.

He pedaled on, keeping an eye out for the truant officer, park rangers, cops, his mom's friends, or anyone else who might bust him. He also had to keep track of time and maintain a good pace. He needed to hit all the areas while the tide permitted, then pedal up to the marina, get his pay, and return at three-twenty in the afternoon, when he would normally get home from school. It was a lot to keep straight throughout the day, but he managed. Besides, it was a hell of a lot more fun than Social Studies or Math.

Luckily, the shoreline was deserted, except for the seabirds. Gulls cruised on the breeze, screeching at each other. Danny hated the sound of gulls. Last summer he and his friends had fed them Alka-Seltzer to see if their stomachs would really explode. One of the birds dropped out of the sky, landed at his feet, and croaked a white bubbling death rattle onto his sneakers. The others had laughed, while Danny hid his horror and revulsion. He didn't let them see him cry. Danny still felt bad about the gull, but would never admit it to his friends.

Especially Jeremy. He could be mean. Matt and Chuck usually sided with Danny. Ronnie usually went along with Jeremy. And sometimes, Jeremy didn't behave like a friend. Still, he was part of The Hill Crew, and kids from The Hill always stuck together—as it had always been. *Someone* had to look out for them. Their parents certainly wouldn't. None of their parents were worth a crap, so they looked out for each other. Jeremy was a good friend to have. He never ratted you out. Never let anyone screw you over. But beneath his surface was a frightful temper, always at a full-boil. When the gull died at Danny's feet, Jeremy laughed until he almost split a gut. The triumph in Jeremy's eyes made Danny sick. The way he said, "Fuck yeah! Let's do it again!" scared him.

The surf droned. The gulls continued screeching. Danny watched the frenzied birds. He noticed they were hovering over one particular section of the water. When he saw why, he almost wrecked the bike.

"Holy shit!"

He hit the brake. Gravel and dust plumed from the Schwinn's back tire. The insects in the trees lining the path fell silent. Nature held its breath. Even the gulls suddenly seemed quiet. The only sounds were the waves lapping against the stony beach and the sharp clicking of crab shells.

Danny gaped. He'd never seen so many crabs in one place. Not in the tanks at the aquarium, or the seafood restaurants his father used to take him to.

Blinding flashes of sunlight gleamed off their shells as they jostled each other, a huge pile of scurrying segmented legs and clacking claws five feet out into the shallow water. Hundreds of them, right there for the picking. Danny's heart beat faster. If he was quick enough, he could fill the bucket, pedal like mad up to Haverstraw, get another bucket there, and come back to grab the remainder.

Jackpot.

His salvation, the YZ-125, was within reach. Right here, right *now*. He could drive it home today. Home? Why bother driving there? With the dirt bike, he could go *anywhere.* He could be in Jersey in less than half an hour if he took the service road by the train tracks—or so people said. He'd never been down that far himself.

He dismounted the Schwinn and hurried over to the skittering pile. As he approached, Danny realized the tide would come in by the time he rode to Haverstraw and back. If that happened, the crabs would be gone. He needed to get all that he could now, but he had only the single bucket and it wasn't large enough. He sure wasn't going to *carry* an armload of live, angry blue crabs to Haverstraw.

Shit.

He needed a bigger bucket. Or a cooler. Or a backhoe, freight train, tractor trailer. Danny looked around the shore and saw broken glass, cigarette butts, a discarded condom—but nothing useful.

Shit!

Further up the bike path was a small picnic area with unkempt grass around the picnic table and a stone barbeque. The garbage can overflowed with beer bottles, paper plates, and hot dog package wrappers, but he could dump all that and wash the stink out in the river. It would be a bitch dragging the can all the way up to Haverstraw once it was full, but he figured he could manage, if it brought him closer to his dirt bike...and if it took longer than expected and he got home late, who cared? This was worth getting busted for.

Assuming he got paid before being caught.

Bees and ants swarmed the garbage can. Danny upturned it onto the grass and shooed the more persistent bees. He dragged it down toward the pile of crabs and winced. Something stank. Not just the Hudson or the garbage can. This was something else. Like something had died nearby.

Danny plucked the crabs off of each other, avoiding their snapping claws. He felt something moist and spongy on his fingertips. It repulsed him, that single touch. The stench grew stronger. He wiped his hand on his shirt and looked down at the skittering pile. The crabs were crawling on something. His vision blurred when he tried to see what it was. He let his eyes un-focus, and then focused again. Danny carefully snatched away two of the largest crabs and stared into a red mess.

The dead body had no eyes to stare back at him with—indeed, it had no face at all.

Danny didn't scream, even when a small crab scrambled out of the corpse's mouth and threatened him with one angrily waving claw. Instead, he stared—surprise, confusion, disbelief. A dead man, dressed in an orange jumpsuit. The scavengers had picked off much of the exposed flesh. Raw, red patches had replaced hair and skin. Yellow clumps of fat waved in the shallow water. Between the mass of crabs were glimpses of bone. Danny couldn't tear his eyes away. He could see into the throat; watched crabs pick at the inside of the chest. They jammed choice clippings of lung tissue into their tiny mouths. Others scurried under the orange jumpsuit.

Above him, the gulls began to shriek again.

He'd found a dead body.

Holy crap! His mind started catching up to the situation. Orange jumpsuit, like the kind they wore in…

Danny glanced across the river. New York's most infamous prison stared back at him from the other side, white and foreboding and eerily silent. Sing Sing—home of Ol' Sparky, the electric chair.

There had been an escape yesterday. It was all over the news but he'd paid more attention to the rumors at school. The escaped con, a murderer, was the brother of Mr. Bedrik, Danny's teacher. Nobody knew how he'd gotten free. It was like he'd vanished from his cell. And the authorities couldn't find him, either. Nobody could. Not until now. Could this be him? It had to be. How many other dead bodies in prison inmate uniforms were lying on the bank? It had to be Mr. Bedrik's brother. But it was hard to tell. The corpse's features looked more like strips of raw bacon than human.

Danny flinched as another crab swatted at him. He had to tell Matt, Ronnie, Chuck, and Jeremy. After they saw it, he would call the cops, but he had to show them first. Otherwise they would never believe him, think he made the whole thing up. But *shit!*—they were all still at school.

School! Oh, crap.

If he called the cops, he'd have to explain his truancy and what brought him to the river in the first place. If he told them he was selling crabs, they would tell his mom, and if *she* found out that he had almost enough money for a dirt bike, she would steal the cash and drink it all, leaving him with nothing. And he'd get in trouble for skipping school, too.

In Jeremy's immortal words, *fuck that noise.*

So he had two choices. He could either wait until the guys got out of school to show them, or get the hell out of here with his crabs and pretend like it never happened. Maybe the corpse would be safe until then. If so, then he could report the discovery and get the credit. Be on the nightly news. Be the talk of school the next day. Maybe there was a reward, too. The guy was an escaped convict, after all.

If he left now, someone else might find the body and get all the credit.

There had to be a way to sell the crabs, take credit for discovering the body, show his friends before the cops, and not get busted for skipping school again. Before he could formulate a plan, footsteps approached him from behind.

Danny turned. The weird Russian guy, Gustav, glided toward him. Gustav was

Brackard's Point's resident oddity. Jeremy said that Gustav was queer, but Jeremy said a lot of things—always talking shit. Gustav's age was undetermined—somewhere between his mid-forties and late sixties. A thick, long beard obscured much of his face. He wore a weather-beaten coat and baggy, threadbare jeans with a hole in one knee. His dirty work boots echoed with each step. One hand was in his coat pocket. The other clutched a cigarette butt tied to a piece of string. The old man held the string out in front of him as he walked. The butt spun like a miniature propeller.

As Gustav approached, the blue crabs scattered, abandoning their feast. The gulls above continued to circle and shriek.

Danny's legs felt frozen, his mind numb.

Gustav drew closer, and the cigarette butt spun towards Danny. The concentric circles grew smaller. Then it stopped swinging altogether. Gustav looked up, saw Danny standing over the dead body and the fleeing crabs, and stopped.

I am so busted.

The old Russian blinked at him, inquisitive.

Danny offered a smile. "Hi...Umm...Look what I found."

The smile was not returned. Saying nothing, Gustav stuffed the string and the cigarette butt in his pocket, and scratched his bearded chin. He gave the body a cursory glance as if it were no more than litter on the freeway, but studied Danny intently. At first, he appeared confused. As the moments passed, he seemed angry, amused, annoyed, and saddened. Finally, he spoke.

"Here you are."

Danny didn't reply immediately because he was not sure if it was a question or a summation. He looked down at his feet. The crabs—and his dirt bike—scurried away on segmented legs. When Gustav said nothing further, Danny finally stammered, "I—I was just..."

Ignoring him, Gustav bent down over the corpse. He looked from the body to Danny, and then back again. He shook his head and muttered in Russian, then reached for Danny's shoulder to pull himself up.

Danny took a step backward. "I—I found him."

"Did you?" Gustav arched an eyebrow. He motioned for Danny to help him rise.

Danny didn't move.

"Come," Gustav grumbled. "Help an old man to his feet."

Danny complied. Gustav slapped dirt from his knees, and looked at Danny.

"Did you, indeed?"

"Yeah, I did. I mean, what—you think I killed him?"

Gustav laughed. Overhead, the gulls screeched in chorus. Glaring at the flock, he muttered something under his breath. Immediately, the circling birds fell silent.

"Now we will not be interrupted. Do I think you killed him? Nyet."

"Huh?"

"Nyet. No. You do not kill. Not yet."

Danny frowned. Was the last "nyet" or "not yet"? He knew what it *sounded* like, but it made no sense.

"What's wrong, boy?"

"You said, 'Did you?' like you didn't believe me when I said I found him."

Gustav nodded. "That is because you did not find him."

"I swear! I didn't *put* him here or anything. He was laying there under all the crabs, I just—"

Gustav waved his hand, silencing him.

"He was not meant to be found by anyone. The body was hidden in plain sight. You did not find him. He found *you.*"

"Found me?" Danny forced himself to laugh. "Come on. That's crazy."

"Crazy?" Gustav plucked three long hairs from the dead man's head. "Crazy, you say. Madness. Yes. Yes, it is. But true? Oh... perhaps? Perhaps that also, no?"

Danny blinked, watching in revulsion.

Gustav chuckled as he braided the three hairs into a tiny rope.

"I...I don't understand what you mean. And what are you doing with his hair?"

"What do you like to be called, boy?"

"Danny."

"Okay, Danny. And I like to be called Gustav."

"I know who you are."

"Do you?" The Russian pinched the braid of hair in his left hand. It fluttered in the breeze. With his right hand, Gustav fished a pack of cigarettes out of his coat pocket. He offered one to the boy.

"You accept my offering, yes?"

Shrugging, Danny took it. Gustav slid a chrome Zippo lighter with a strange symbol on it from his pocket. He held it out for Danny's smoke, and then lit his own. As he exhaled, he looked deep into Danny's eyes. Danny wondered if the old man was a pervert. Maybe Jeremy had been right about him.

"Uh…thanks." Danny took a drag.

The aroma of tobacco filled the air, momentarily blocking out the dead man's stench. This was the first time Danny had smoked in front of an adult. Usually, it was with his friends. They'd sneak cigarettes from their parents' cartons and smoke them on top of Hook Mountain, flicking the butts off the cliff, hoping that no one down below would recognize them and tell their parents. All of their parents subscribed to "Do as I say, not as I do."

"You're welcome."

Gustav nodded at the braided rope of hair in his fingertips. It bent toward Danny. Danny considered accusing the Russian of making the hair do that, somehow manipulating it with his fingertips in imperceptible movements, but he knew better. It was like the spinning cigarette butt when Gustav approached, the silencing of the gulls and the banishment of the crabs to their rocky hidey-holes—a whole bunch of shit that shouldn't be, but was regardless.

Crazy shit...*but true?*

Gustav coughed. "Yes. You begin to understand now."

"No. I actually don't."

"Actually?"

"Yes, actually. I don't understand *anything* you just said."

Gustav flicked the Zippo and touched the flame to the hair. It flared bright in his hand, intense and white. It took a moment to fade, leaving purple blotches in his vision. The smell filled Danny's nostrils, powerful even over the cigarette and the corpse.

"You do not understand? You do not know?"

Danny breathed through his mouth. "I said I don't."

"You know much." Gustav grinned. "Much. You just don't know it yet."

The sun moved higher in the sky.

The corpse had two shadows, but Danny didn't notice.

Two

MICHAEL BEDRIK WALKED along the path through Gethsemane Cemetery, chuckling to himself.

A man—a boy, really—clad in a pretentious amount of black sat on one of the benches. He drew in a sketch pad. His model was unaware. She sat fifty feet away against one of the graves, engaged in an internal guilt-ridden conversation with her dead sister.

The artist had convinced himself that he was a tragic romantic. As he drew, he entertained a fantasy of shyly presenting his work to her and introducing himself. She, being both intrigued and flattered, would agree to a cup of coffee with him at the café on the corner. Following the coffee, they would have a deep, intellectually stimulating conversation, then a slow sensuous fucking amongst many pillows and red satin sheets.

Bedrik stopped in front of the kid. The boy looked up, his face like one of the concrete angels on the family tombs; manipulated and false.

"May I help you?" His eyes still swam with erotic fantasy.

Bedrik stuck his hands in his pockets. "No."

Then he walked away.

"Asshole," the kid whispered, careful not to let the man hear him.

But Bedrik did, and he smiled.

Michael Bedrik cast no shadow.

He turned left at the next intersection, up the hill toward the girl. For a moment, he worried about the kid drawing him into the scene on his sketchpad, but the kid was far too self-absorbed in his fantasies to include another man in his drawing. The artist wanted no rivals, even if they could be easily erased. So beat the passive hearts of the weak-willed.

Bedrik strolled amongst the stones. He passed the family tomb of a musician from the State Philharmonic; the headstone of the Harborview Diner's original owner; the individual graves of convicted murderer Francis Dwight Lundgren's victims; the marker for the unnamed homeless man found frozen behind the lumber yard last winter; senior citizens; infants; children; thieves; preachers; police officers; town selectmen; war heroes; dozens more. Saints and sinners. Losers and winners. Each grave in Gethsemane told a story. All one had to do was listen.

The girl didn't notice his passing. She was busy apologizing to her dead sister. Two rows down, Bedrik stopped and knelt down in front of a grave. The marble stone indicated that it was the final resting place of Edward T. Rammel. Names were power. He did not know the name on the stone, but noted it anyway. The dates meant nothing to him. He gave them only a cursory glance. Only the name mattered. The name—and the restlessness he felt emanating from beneath the earth. Whoever Edward T. Rammel was, he did not want to be dead. He'd died angry. Too young for his liking, but most people felt that in the end. In Michael Bedrik's experience, graveyards were full of those that died too young. Ask any of them, and they'd tell you the same. They were gypped, robbed, cut down in their prime by disease, disaster, discontent.

Bedrik chuckled. The bitchings of the dead were like the bitchings of imprisoned men. Across the river in Sing Sing, everyone was innocent. Ask them and they'd tell you. They were set up, victims of circumstance and prejudice, accident of birth, wrong place, wrong time, disaster, discontentment.

Prison or cemetery; they were the same thing, really. But there were no breakouts from the latter.

At least, very few. Bedrik planned to change that. Edward T. Rammel was going to be the first. The first of many. Bedrik knew his name. Felt his anger. That was all he needed. That gave him the power.

And magic was all about power.

Bedrik stood up and brushed the grass from his pants. He wandered amongst the tombstones, attuned to the clamoring beneath his feet. Soon, the girl left. The artist slinked after her like a wounded spaniel begging his master's forgiveness for pissing the rug. The sun followed them both, leaving Bedrik alone in the cemetery. Night fell. Solitude engulfed him—the one exception being the restless dead.

He heard them call out; beg for release in frustrated, pitiful tones for lack of anything else to do. Most did not expect an answer, feared they would never receive one.

"I'll be back for the rest of you," he whispered. "But for now, I can take only one. Rules are rules, after all."

Off in the distance, a small yellow-green light flashed weakly. Then another, a few feet away, then some more further toward the wall, near the trees. Lightning bugs. Miniature will o' wisps pulsing in the near-summer night.

As a child, Bedrik had collected them in Mason jars, poking holes in the lid so they could breathe. Then he learned to smash their bellies and paint his skin with their guts so that he, too, would glow in the dark.

Just like names, innards contained power.

Bedrik held out his hands and whispered a word. Then he bit down on the inside of his cheek. Blood filled his mouth. He spat the blood onto the grave. Bedrik waited, ignoring the taste in the back of his throat.

The lightning bugs came to him. They were not swift fliers, but he'd had long years to learn patience. Every few seconds, the lights in their bellies flashed, the duration becoming longer, the intensity brighter as more bugs joined together to fly in tight formation. By the time the horde of insects reached him, it traveled as a pulsing ball of yellow light, bright enough to make him squint. Shielding his eyes with his hand, Bedrik spoke another word and the pulsing stopped. The glare stayed steady, hovering before him. He pointed, and the light followed his direction, coming to rest a few feet over Edward T. Rammel's grave.

Bedrik watched.

A shadow appeared on the ground, right on top of the grave. The shadow turned its head, inspecting its form—the dark suggestions of torso, arms, and legs. It rose as only shadows could—projecting itself onto small clods of grave-dirt, blades of grass, its own headstone. The shade turned to look at its epitaph, then back at Bedrik.

Bedrik looked at the shadow and said, "I bind you, Edward T. Rammel. Your shade will do my bidding, as my own."

The black shape stared at him with unseen eyes.

"You wanted out of there," Bedrik explained. "This is the only way I could help you. Trust me. You'll come to enjoy it. This is your lucky day."

The shadow knelt before him and sobbed. Invisible tears of gratitude fell, swallowed by the unforgiving night.

"Come," Bedrik said. "We've much to do, you and I."

Bedrik walked out of the cemetery and down the street. The shadow followed in his footsteps. The streets were crowded, but no one noticed them. No one noticed that Bedrik's shadow seemed to be a bit darker than others or that it did not follow his movements exactly, that it would, at times, reach out to stroke a woman's hair, or pause before a store window that did not exist when it was alive. No one noticed that the lightning bugs in Gethsemane Cemetery were hovering over the grave of Edward T. Rammel in one large cluster. No one noticed anything was amiss because Bedrik wished it.

People had such narrow worldviews. They lived their unimportant lives, believed they knew what to do with them, believed they could separate truth from lie and in so doing, live well according to the parameters of a society they did not understand. They looked out on the world through a soda-straw perspective. If the reality could not be fully seen in their microvision, then it was discredited, debunked, and denied. Such was the mentality of the populous today, as it was in millennia past, and would be eons into the future. People were stupid. That truth was as absolute as death and taxes; it was not going to change.

In fact, people like Bedrik counted on it.

Bedrik knew all too well how stupid men were; his brother Martin, for example. So desperate for recognition from his sibling that he'd volunteered to place himself in harm's way to gain a modicum of Bedrik's respect. The respect was not forthcoming, but his brother's fate was grievous. Death usually was.

Martin Bedrik was the *bad* twin. All his life, he was the case study. He got caught doing things. He made poor choices. Rebelled against his situation of birth; tried to establish himself as an individual, a separate entity from his brother. When they were in high school, Martin got into fights, and was caught selling coke and pot. He was always in trouble for something or another. Michael joined the chess club, played cello in the school orchestra, and was on the yearbook staff. He was sociable and extroverted and got along easily with not only his fellow students, but also the teachers and administrators.

Michael never spoke ill about his identical twin, but he never said much good about him either, and no one blamed him for doing so. No one, except Martin. The older they grew, the more Martin got into trouble, and the more often he lamented his miserable existence compared to his brother's gifted one. When he was at his lowest points, drunk and maudlin, Martin would bemoan the lack of respect he felt he had always received from Michael.

When Martin crossed from misdemeanors into felonies, and graduated from county jail to the state penitentiary, Michael began visiting him. Talked with him. Bestowed kindness, the miniscule favors one could give to a state-housed convicted felon. It didn't take long before Martin viewed his brother as a god and savior. He'd do anything his twin asked of him.

"Well," Michael said one day, staring through the thick glass partition separating them. "There is something you could do, actually."

"What?"

"It doesn't matter. Not while you're in here."

"I won't be getting out for a while. Not this time."

"I know," Michael said. His sympathy was a reasonable facsimile of genuine.

"So throw it by me," Martin said. "What could it hurt?"

"There's no point," Michael said. "It's not something we could do anyway."

"Whadda ya mean, *we*?" The thought of doing something—anything—with his brother brought Martin too much hope. His hope was his weakness, and Michael preyed on that. Martin played his hand too early. The pitiful thing was that he had no idea he'd already lost the game.

"They're listening," Michael said. "We'll talk about this later. Okay?"

Martin looked into his brother's eyes—the mirror of his own.

Get me out of here, he thought, and I'll do whatever you want.

"You take it easy," Michael said. "I'll come back soon as I can."

He placed the phone in its cradle and stood up.

Martin pressed his palm against the glass. Don't leave me in here. Please, don't let me rot in this shit-hole.

Just before Michael turned to exit, he locked on to his brother's stare and responded in kind: *I won't.*

His mouth never moved, but Martin had heard him anyway.

A car horn blew, bringing Bedrik back to the present.

He'd kept his promise. He hadn't let Martin rot in that shit-hole. Instead, Michael had let Martin rot on the beach, after binding his own shadow to Martin's corpse.

Bedrik adjusted the chain around his neck. His fingers traveled down and touched the symbol hanging upon it, then over his chest. He remembered that the shadow following him that was not his own. Self-consciousness got the better of him. His hand dropped to his side, swinging along with his gait.

Behind him, the shadow's hand did the same.

He'd bought the house and moved to Brackard's Point a year ago. He'd taken a job at the school, was polite, did his best to fit in, and kept to himself. Bedrik's home was no different from the rest of the middle-class neighborhood. It was a raised-ranch style, and sported the typical vinyl siding, *faux* shutters. The root system of a large maple tree had cracked his sidewalk about three-fifths of the way down. Most of the homes in the older developments such as this had similar minimal flaws. Real estate agents called these defects "character." Homeowners maintained the rose-tint perception, too proud to admit fault.

In the autumn, Bedrik's maple leaves stayed only a few days before disappearing. The grass was trimmed, with few dandelions or crabgrass, and only the occasional unhealthy spot. It was not immaculate, but it wasn't an eyesore. He could have made it lush and weed-free with a few whispered words and a few scattered ingredients, but that might have attracted attention. His mailbox looked like any other, his driveway nondescript. It was on the swell of the bell curve—so average as to be invisible. When the neighbors compared yards, his was mentioned only because of the maple. If they discussed his house at all, the only thing they came up with was that no one could recall seeing Mr. Bedrik lift a finger to maintain the place.

To his neighbors, Michael Bedrik was just another drone. He preferred it that way. He'd return a smile or wave, engage in meaningless chit-chat, gripe about the potholes on Pensie Avenue, politely bitch about politicians, but that was all. He was recognized, but not known, for none of his neighbors could comprehend the presence of such a man in their midst.

In order to see Bedrik for what he was, one would have to know some things—certain truths, certain lies...see through certain illusions, dismiss certain pretences. All far beyond the capacity of the plebes. Bedrik was an extraordinary man, and it would take another extraordinary man to identify him, his power and position. And extraordinary men, by definition, were scarce.

Gustav could have identified him, but Bedrik had masked his presence from the old man—so far. He would save Gustav for last.

His neighbors knew nothing about him, but he knew everything about them. Things they didn't even know about themselves. He knew their names—the secret names given to them long before they were born. He knew their sins and trespasses, their signs and sigils. All they knew about him was what he wished them to know.

"I have something for you to do," Bedrik told the shadow. "I'm going to give you a new lease on life. Tonight, you must pay a visit to Tony Amiratti Junior."

The shade listened.

Danny took another cigarette from Gustav. "What do you mean, he found me?"

"You are a smart boy. You know things without ever being taught them, no?"

Danny looked away. Gustav's words made him uncomfortable, as did the old man's stare.

"Yes," Gustav continued. "You know things. I know this because I know things too."

"Jeremy was right about you. You're weird."

"Yes. I am. You are too, no? Many kids at school make fun of you behind your back. They do this because they're afraid of you. Why?"

Danny shrugged. "Because of my friends? I don't know why they're scared of me. But Matt, Jeremy, Ronnie, and Chuck are pretty tough."

"Your friends...Perhaps, but I think not. I think it is *you* who frighten them more than your friends."

"Why, though?"

"Because you know things. You can know things about your classmates... their nightmares."

"I don't know anything about them."

"Ah, but you do, you do. You know things about them intuitively; it's second nature, yes? You are not always aware that you know these things, yet know them you do—and well. Understand?"

"No, not really." But Danny's dismissal had little heart.

"Not really, you say. Really, yes, you do, but you choose not to see your talents for the sake of your friends. They would think differently of you, yes? So you play dumb to make them feel better."

"What do you mean?"

"Your friends. You all pretend you're dumber than you are as to not offend each other. It would not be seemly for one of you to excel intellectually; such is against your sensibilities."

"Don't be calling my friends dumb, you crazy old Commie bastard. President Reagan is gonna take care of you guys! Just wait and see."

Gustav sighed, and took the string out of his pocket. He plucked the still-burning cigarette from Danny's lips and quickly tied it to the end opposite the other butt, then extended his index finger. When he laid the string on his fingertip, it began to rotate, spinning like a propeller.

Danny's anger vanished. "How are you doing that?"

"Stick your finger out."

Hesitant, Danny offered his index finger. The spinning cigarette butts floated from Gustav's finger to Danny's. The speed of rotation increased, and the butts were a bit wobbly, but after a moment they stabilized.

"How the hell are you doing that?" Danny asked again. The butts quit spinning and lay limp at the ends of the string. "Hey! Why'd you make it stop?"

Gustav smiled. "Me? I wasn't controlling it. You were."

"No." Danny shook his head. "There's just no way. I don't know how to do that."

"It quit spinning when you questioned yourself. No?"

"Oh, come on," Danny said.

"So hard to believe in yourself, is it? Is easy to dismiss all that's happened to chance?"

"You're still saying this dead guy was looking for me?"

"Perhaps he was calling for you. Looking for you, he was. I was. Lots of people are looking for you."

"Like the truancy officer, *maybe*," Danny said. "But anyone else? C'mon. No one gives a shit about me. Mom couldn't care less. Now, seriously—how did you do that?"

"Again, I did not. You did."

"I don't know what you're talking about."

"Maybe I'm talking about your future."

"My future? What's that supposed to mean?"

"Come," Gustav said. "I would show you things. Things you need to know, yes? Come...come."

He started walking away from the corpse, toward the trail. He did not turn around.

"What about him?" Danny pointed at the corpse. "Shouldn't we call someone?"

Gustav looked back at the body, then back up to Danny. "Now that he found you, others can find him soon enough. Understand?"

"Not really."

Gustav turned away again and continued walking.

"What about my bike?"

"It is taken care of," the old man called over his shoulder. "No one will find it."

"But it's lying out here in the open."

"There are many things in plain sight that cannot be seen. Just like that dead man was."

With one last glance at his Schwinn, Danny followed Gustav, giving only a passing thought to the half-eaten body in the water. He thought more about the crabs he didn't catch, the silent gulls, and how Gustav made the string spin. Try as he might, he could not get the string to stay on the end of his finger. It slipped off with each step he took. Danny tried slowing his pace to keep steadier but that didn't help much either, though it did manage to stay on his fingertip for a fraction of a second longer.

Five steps ahead, Gustav muttered something under his breath.

"What'd you say?" Danny asked, hurrying to catch up.

"So hard you try. Too hard, perhaps?"

"You always answer a question with a question?"

"Questions...you must dare to ask, and learn. Too simple is it to be told answers. They become...invaluable, see? That which *you* put together in *your* mind...this is true learning. This is *understanding,* yes? Repeating answers by rote...good for parrots. They get crackers. Bad for boys. Bad for men."

"That's all they want at school," Danny said. "That's why I hate the place."

Gustav frowned. "Hate the place, or the learning?"

"They don't teach us anything...they just... recite, you know? And they want you to spit it back at them same way they said it to you."

"This I understand. You understand, too. Question, question, and question some more. Every question leads to a better question, until there can only be silence as an answer."

Danny's face scrunched up. "I think I get you."

"Good. Then you begin to understand."

They walked on in silence.

...and the string spun.

THREE

DANNY HAD NEVER seen so many books. Every room, every wall, floor to ceiling bookshelves, and not a single one was empty. Danny tried to read their spines, but it was too dark. The lights were off and the windows were blocked.

"Can you turn the lights on?" Danny asked.

Gustav clapped his hands. The lights came on.

"How'd you do that?" Danny asked.

"How?" Gustav grinned. "Guess."

"I don't know; some kind of weird shit, like the string?"

"Perhaps. Yes, perhaps that. Or perhaps not."

"Well, what else would it be?"

"Maybe from the television, yes? You've seen the commercials? $19.95, plus shipping and handling. They double your order—for free! Can you believe? Act now and get a special bonus gift."

Danny clapped his hands, and the lights turned off. He clapped them again and they went back on. "I can't believe you actually ordered that thing. Everyone knows the stuff they sell on TV is a ripoff."

Shrugging, Gustav walked over to a shelf, selected a book, and placed it in Danny's hand.

"Read."

Danny looked at the cover. It was blank. He flipped it over; the same. He opened it, turned a few pages. They were also blank. "There's nothing here."

Gustav clapped his hands. The lights went out.

"Hey," Danny yelled. "Turn them back on!"

"No."

"Turn them on, man. I'm warning you, if you try anything I'll—"

"You talk too much. Read."

"I can't read if I can't *see*, you crazy old commie!" Danny put the book down and clapped his hands to turn the lights back on.

Nothing happened.

He clapped them again. The darkness remained.

"Great, now that piece of shit As-Seen-On-TV thing you bought is busted."

"Stop that."

Danny tried clapping again. No lights. The darkness seemed to swell, as if it were pressing against him.

"Stop," Gustav said. "Sit down. Read."

"I told you, I can't read in the dark."

"No?"

"Of course not."

"Why?"

Danny sighed. "You need light to see, stupid. And besides, there wasn't anything in that book. It's blank."

"You're sure?"

"Sure of what?"

"Of everything."

"I'm sure there was nothing in there, I'm sure you need light to see, and I'm sure that the stupid thing you bought ain't—"

Danny clapped his hands

"—fucking—"

clap, clap

"—working!"

Gustav clapped and the light came on. He extended his hand. "Give me the book."

Danny handed it to him.

"Stand on the chair," Gustav said.

"What?"

"Stand on the chair."

Danny grew nervous. "What for?"

Gustav said nothing. He stared at Danny, frowning.

"Fine," Danny groaned. "I'll stand on the frigging chair if it'll make you happy. But then I got to get going. I can't believe I came here."

"Look at the light."

Danny glanced at it. "Yeah. It's a light. Big whoop."

"Wait there." Gustav left the room. Danny heard him open a closet door. He returned, carrying a light bulb. "You see? Sixty watts. Should be brighter, no?"

Danny shrugged. "What's in there now?"

"Take it out. You tell me."

Danny licked his fingertips, and touched the bulb. He was surprised. It was cool, not hot. He unscrewed it. The bulb came free of the socket...

...and glowed in his hand.

"How the..."

Clap, clap.

The light turned off in his hand.

Clap, clap.

Back on.

Danny was speechless. Gustav stopped clapping and fell silent again. Turning the glowing bulb over in his hands, Danny looked for a battery or an ultra-thin wire that he might have missed, but found neither. His mouth dropped open. There was no battery. No spider-silk-thin wire. No As-Seen-On-TV offer mechanism hooked up to the house lights. It was...

Like the spinning string.

Like the crabs. The gulls.

...impossible?

"Put it back," Gustav said.

Danny screwed the light back in.

"Sit down."

Danny sat.

"Read."

Clap, clap.

The light went out again. Danny stared at the empty page, trying to wrap his head around all that had just happened. He saw nothing, between the darkness and the empty pages, but still he sat, looking at the book, trying to come to terms with the series of bizarre events. His mind replayed the whole day, the things that Gustav had said, the things he'd done... things that seemed impossible...but mostly, Danny thought of the string spinning on his own finger.

What was possible, really?

Anything? Everything?

His vision blurred. When it cleared, he saw that a series of strange symbols had appeared on the blank page.

Gustav squeezed his shoulder. "You see now, yes?"

"I see it, but I don't understand it."

"Of course you can't understand that book," Gustav said. "Never seen the language before, no?"

"Right. So why'd you give me this when I can't read it?"

"I gave you the book to prove to you the light. It can only be read in darkness."

"It's some kind of invisible ink that glows in the dark, right?"

"Is it?"

Danny started to agree that it was, but deep down inside, he knew better. This was something else entirely. "Are all the books like this?"

"Like what?"

Danny hesitated. He knew the word, but it sounded wrong, foolish. Stupid. His friends would have laughed at him. But it was the only word he could think of.

"Magic."

"All books are magic," Gustav said. "Now try again. Try to read."

"I can't—"

"No. There is no 'can't,' understand?"

"You sound like a Russian Yoda."

"What is this 'Yoda'?"

"Are you serious? You don't know?"

"Nyet."

"What?"

"Nyet. No. Explain."

"He's a Jedi master. Sort of looks like a frog."

"Bah." Gustav waved his hand in dismissal. "Read."

Danny tried making sense of the symbols on the page, looking for a pattern.

"*Now* you're trying," Gustav said. "Yes, *now* you see."

"Shut up," Danny said. "I'm trying to read this."

Gustav said no more. He watched as Danny engrossed himself in the book. Watched as the afternoon passed and turned to evening, and then to night. Watched as, outside, the shadows started to dance.

He stared into the darkness, and the darkness stared back.

FOUR

DANA WHEELER KNEW how to use her looks. Her biggest problem was a lack of ambition. She could have gone on to bigger and better things on her own, but she preferred being with the right guys who might take her to bigger and better things themselves.

Currently, the right guy was Tony Amiratti Junior. As far as the public knew, his dad owned a roofing company, an electronics store, and invested heavily in the right stocks. In reality, Tony Amiratti Senior was part of the Marano Family crime syndicate. So was Tony Junior. Like father like son. As a result, Tony had money to spend on Dana. They lived the good life. All she had to do was make sure he stayed satisfied—and she was very good at keeping Tony happy. Much better than the other women he slept with.

Sweat glistened on her naked body. Her nipples hardened as the ceiling fan gently blew air across them. Tony snored softly.

Dana was restless and wide-awake. Tony never had that problem after sex. He needed a full night to recover. She didn't really mind, but now and then it would have been nice to talk afterwards. She glanced at the alarm clock on the dresser. Nine PM. Not late. Sleep would be a long time coming.

The bathroom light was on. Its rays spilled out from the open door and into the bedroom, casting shadows. Movement in the corner of the room caught her attention, and she looked to her right. There was nothing to see, but the fine hairs on her arm rose. One of the shadows seemed darker than the others.

"Tony? Baby?"

Tony mumbled in his sleep.

Dana had always been afraid of the dark. Bad things waited in the shadows. That's what her older brother Pete used to say when they were kids. He'd told her that shadows had minds of their own. Growing up, she'd believed him. As an adult, the notion was easy to dismiss.

It wasn't so easy now.

Tony rolled over and smacked his lips. "Tell Vince to ugh wump," he mumbled. Then he was silent again.

Dana was about to dismiss her nervousness when, in the darkness, something moved again. She sat up. A shadow slipped across the wall and glided slowly along the carpet. The bathroom light did not keep the shadow at bay. She tried to cry out, but couldn't. As she watched, the shadow slipped up over the foot of the bed. It was human in size and shape, but there was no one else in the room with them. Dana blinked her eyes. Her stomach knotted with old childhood fears. Her brother's voice taunted her.

She moaned.

The shadow hovered over Tony, settling on him, covering the length of his body. Gasping, he awoke suddenly, jolting upright. His eyes were wide. His mouth opened and closed like a fish.

Terrified, Dana slipped off the side of the bed and landed on the thick carpet. "Tony? Oh God..."

Tony reached for her, his eyes growing wider. Dana jumped to her feet, reaching for the light switch. Tony began shaking. The bedsprings squeaked. And then Dana screamed.

The shadow pushed Tony down onto the bed again and wrapped its hands around his neck. Dana saw finger-shaped indentations on the flesh of Tony's neck as the shadow squeezed, even though the attacker's fingers were indeterminable. The shadow shoved Tony's face into the mattress. Tony's hands clenched the sheets and beat against the bed. Dana moved closer, grabbing at the shadow. Her fingers slid through the darkness, feeling nothing but a sudden wave of cold.

One of the shadow's hands released Tony's neck and sought her instead. Its cold grasp brushed her face and hair while Tony desperately sucked in a breath of air and gagged. Dana screamed again. The shadow took advantage. Its hand slid into her open mouth. The darkness slipped past her lips, her teeth, and pushed into her throat. It pushed into Tony's mouth as well. Dana had one advantage over her lover—she was still on her feet. She staggered backwards. The shadow stretched like taffy for a moment before losing its hold on her. The frigid, inky substance left her mouth and air rushed in to fill the void. Dana retched. Tony made a small, choking sound.

Without looking back, Dana ran, taking the hallway in four strides, bouncing off the wall as she dashed into the living room. The house was dark, filled with more shadows, more places where bad things could hide. Dana froze, uncertain if she wanted to go further. But she couldn't go back into the bedroom. The house was silent now, but she had no doubt what was happening back the way she'd come. She slapped her hand against the wall, feeling for the light switch. A framed picture of Tony's grandmother fell to the floor. Glass shattered at her bare feet. Even though she couldn't see, she knew the location of the picture. It was the only one in the room. She had to go at least six more feet before she'd reach the front door. Dana stepped forward, forgetting about the broken glass. A shard punched through the bottom of her foot.

"Fuck!" Her voice cracked. She tottered on one foot. Again, her fingers sought the light switch.

She found something else instead.

A hand closed over hers. It was warm, not cold, and flesh, not shadow. Dana tried to pull back, but the hand squeezed harder until she thought her fingers would break.

"Your brother was right, Dana," a male voice whispered in her ear. "Bad things do wait in the shadows."

The speaker wasn't familiar. How could he know about her brother, she wondered?

"Tony…"

"He'll be fine. Don't worry about him. Worry about yourself. Now sleep."

Another hand closed over her mouth and the speaker whispered a word Dana didn't understand. She slipped from consciousness.

In Gethsemane Cemetery, the dead cried out, but there was no one around to hear them.

Michael Bedrik received word of his brother's death at a quarter till ten. He'd barely made it home before the police arrived. He hurried up from the basement, wiping his hands on a dishtowel before answering the door. The chief of police, Ed Winters, stood on his porch. Bedrik made sure to look appropriately mournful as the man gave him the news.

"Will you need me to identify the body, Chief Winters?"

"Well, it's really only a formality these days, but in this case, no. He was in the water for a long time, Mr. Bedrik. We were able to identify him through prison dental records, so you don't need to go through that."

Bedrik sighed. "Well, that is a blessing, at least. I don't know how I'd…"

He broke off and wiped his eyes, suppressing the urge to laugh.

Winters looked uncomfortable. "I'm so very sorry for your loss, Mr. Bedrik."

"I appreciate that. Thanks for coming and telling me yourself, Chief. I know it's not the easiest part of your job." He put on the proper expression of grief, not quite getting to tears, but broken up inside, as he shook the man's hand. "I'm afraid it might take me a few hours to make arrangements regarding Martin's"—he made himself choke—"Martin's burial. Is that all right? I don't want to be a nuisance."

"No, really, it's fine. You take all the time you need."

Bedrik knew that Chief Winters hated thinking about the dead. He saw it in his mind. Talking about them was one of the best ways around to drive the man away. Winters had dealt with too many deaths in his own family. Too many loved ones buried before their times were due. It was a side effect of a history of serving the community: One uncle and a father who were both police officers and a brother who chose to be a firefighter. None of them had lived past fifty and the police chief was closing in fast on his forty-ninth birthday. Fear was his constant companion. Bedrik tasted it in the man's aura.

"Thank you again. Be safe on the road, Chief."

"Will do. Take care."

Bedrik smiled. "See you soon, Chief. See you very soon."

After Chief Winters left, Bedrik sat down on the couch and stared at the wall. His amusement turned to anger. Of course he'd known of Martin's death. After all, he'd been responsible.

In order for Bedrik's plan to see fruition, he'd had to anchor his shadow to someone else—a homunculus. But Bedrik had neither the time nor the inclination to build one, to harvest it from his own semen and blood and hair and shape it in the moonlight—not when his twin brother would suffice. Bedrik didn't need to waste his power manufacturing a double. His parents had already manufactured a perfect double for him.

It was easy. He'd simply released Martin from his bonds. One moment, his brother was sleeping in his cell. The next, he was standing alongside the Hudson, staring at Michael in shock, wondering how he'd gotten there and why. Michael answered his brother with a knife. He'd carved sigils that would never be found by the police, because rather than being hewn into Martin's flesh, they'd been carved onto his soul. Then, Bedrik attached his shadow to his brother's corpse. A simple circle of concealment had finished the job, hiding Martin in plain sight, insuring that his brother's corpse wouldn't be found by prying eyes—allowing time for nature to dispose of the evidence. But somehow, that circle had been broken. Martin's body *had* been found.

Bedrik clenched his fists. It should have been flawless. The process had taken only a modicum of power.

Power...

It wasn't an easy thing, the acquisition of power. You could only go so far with your natural talents. After that, if you wanted more, you had to sacrifice and study and wait. Or, if you were Bedrik, you opted for the easier route. Take the power from someone else.

A perfect example was the girl waiting down in the basement.

Sighing, Bedrik stretched and shook his head to clear his exhaustion. It had been a long day and a longer night. There were other forces at work in Brackard's Point. He was sure of it. The discovery of Martin's body proved it. Gustav? Perhaps, but this felt like something more. He couldn't determine what. Still, despite this unforseen occurrence, he'd made some progress. He'd worry about the rest later. No sense wasting power on it now. Wouldn't do for him to be impatient.

He returned to the basement. Dana Wheeler lay naked and spread-eagled across the workbench.

"Hello, Dana. I apologize for the interruption. Where were we?"

Her bloodshot eyes bulged. Her screams were muffled by the strips of duct tape around her mouth. Snot bubbled from her nose.

"None of that," Bedrik stroked her hair. "You have to understand. There are only two ways for me to achieve my goal here. The first would take many years of meditation and offerings, and would hurt me a great deal. The other way—the way I choose—is much quicker and less costly; at least to myself. I only had to give up my shadow, and that didn't hurt at all. You, on the other hand...Well, let's just say this will hurt you much more than it will hurt me."

The knife he took to Dana's flesh was very sharp.

Bedrik whistled while he worked.

When he was finished, he returned to Gethsemane Cemetery, where the shadows rustled with anticipation. He called out to them and the shades answered.

Danny stifled a yawn. He'd read through Gustav's books. Not all of them, but enough to understand more than he'd ever thought possible. Gustav explained that some people had the potential for science and others for magic. They weren't that far apart, really, but at the same time, they were almost opposites. Math had set rules it followed, and they never changed. Magic had rules, too, but they were different for each person. Sometimes they changed a lot. Some rules applied to everyone, and others seemed to be made up as you went along.

"Magic is a part of you," Gustav explained. "You were born that way. You have aptitude, yes? But it is also outside of you. You make magic things happen."

"Is there anything I can't do?"

"Much. But then again, if you had the time..." Gustav shrugged. He seemed sad.

"What do you mean, 'If I had the time'?"

Gustav shook his head. "Is not important. You are young, yes? Will have plenty of time to study and learn. You will do much. All it takes is knowledge and power. That *is* magic—knowledge and power. Knowledge is up to you. Power you can borrow from others."

"Can I fly?"

"Only one way to know, no?"

"Can *you* fly?"

"Sometimes."

"Get the hell out of here. You're telling me you can fly?"

"Yes, but not so good. Not for a long time."

"I wish I could fly."

"Enough of wishes. Wish in one hand. Shit in other. Read."

Danny did his best, but there was so much to take in. There was talk of different levels of reality, of how to travel to them, of other worlds and gods and demons—and things that were neither. Half of what he read seemed like a history lesson, only a lot more interesting than the shit they taught in school. From time to time, he asked Gustav questions. Before the night was done, Danny learned his first spell— how to stop wounds from bleeding. Shortly after midnight, Gustav took the book from him.

"Enough. Go. Come again tomorrow."

"What? But I'm just getting to the good stuff."

"No. No more tonight, Danny. You learn fast. Took me many weeks to learn my first spell but you got it in one day. Go home to your mother now."

Danny stood up. His legs tingled as blood flowed into them again. He'd been sitting for so long, completely lost in the book, and his muscles were stiff. He had to piss, and was hungry and thirsty. But when he saw what time it was, he forgot about all that. He was late. His Mom would be pissed—if she was awake. He bid his new mentor goodbye and headed for home.

The streets were empty, except for the occasional passing car. Danny jogged until his sides ached. Then he stopped. He leaned against an abandoned building, a Greek restaurant that had closed down three years earlier. The boards over the windows were covered with graffiti. Trash littered the sidewalk. Something fluttered above him in the darkness, hidden beyond the reach of the sodium lights; a bird, maybe, or a bat.

Unable to hold it any longer, Danny pulled down his zipper. He shivered with relief. While facing the wall, he heard another noise. It was a faint sound, a distant whisper carried through a long tunnel, only there wasn't a tunnel around. He quickly pulled his zipper up. Then he turned around. The sound continued, but there was nothing to see. Still, there was something out there. He was sure of it. The hairs on the back of his neck rose.

Maybe it's looking for me—whatever it is.

The sound was closer now; shifting, never seeming to be in one place. Danny closed his eyes and tried to think of any of the lessons he'd learned through the night, but nothing seemed coherent.

I spun a fucking string propeller on my fingertip and learned how to stop bleeding! How's that gonna help me now?

The sound changed, snuffling like a dog on the trail of something to eat. Not just any dog, but one like Dusty, the big as sin brute that guarded Silecki's Recycling. Danny knew Dusty from the last time he and his friends had tried sneaking over the fence to collect a few pounds of aluminum to sell back to the cheap bastard. Ronnie had gotten his ass bitten and half the left leg of his jeans torn off before Jeremy nailed the mutt with a rock and made it let go.

For the first time in a very long while, Danny wished for the comfort of his mother. In the shadows, a black shape disengaged from the rest of the darkness and slid towards him. Danny tried to shout, but all that came out was a wheeze. The shadow stretched, reaching for him.

Danny pushed back against the boarded up door of the derelict building. A humming filled his ears, but it wasn't a sound—it was a feeling. The shadow slunk closer. The door vibrated. For one instant, his body felt frozen and burned at the same time. Danny closed his eyes, screamed...

...and then *slid*.

He opened his eyes, gasping in surprise. The restaurant was gone. The shadow was gone. He was home, standing in his living room. He stood pressed up against the wall. His mother was asleep on the sofa, curled up in her nightgown. An empty bottle of tequila on the coffee table told him all he needed to know about her condition. The living room was dark, except for the glow of the television. A guy on Channel 11 was talking about a body found on the banks of the Hudson earlier in the day and how it had been identified as recent prison escapee Martin Bedrik.

Danny shivered from adrenaline rush. He closed his eyes again, trying to calm down. The shadow was gone, whatever it had been, and he was home. All he had to do was figure out how he'd gotten here. Slowly, he smiled. The crappy old restaurant he'd been standing against was six blocks away. It was like he'd been teleported, like on one of those old *Star Trek* shows.

Danny looked at his sleeping mother, and his smile grew wider.

"Magic," he whispered. "Fucking magic."

He checked the garage. His piece of shit bike, the Schwinn which he'd left along the Hudson at Gustav's insistence, leaned against the wall.

Laughing, Danny wondered if he'd done that, too.

Then he wondered what he couldn't do...

By three in the morning, Brackard's Point slept soundly. Hook Mountain watched over the town, a dark and dour sentinel. Lightning flashed on its peak, but no thunder followed. There was no one to witness it anyway. The streets were silent and empty, the homes dark, their curtains drawn. The bell atop the Baptist church rang out with three solemn tolls. Even the hardest of the partiers and drunks were asleep.

But out in the graveyard, the dead were awake, and they talked for those who could listen. Most of it was a litany of pain and suffering, an endless sigh of desperate frustration.

Someone else was awake in the cemetery, too. Sam Oberman walked slowly, playing his flashlight over the tombstones. Sam's philosophy was a nightstick to the head of anyone he caught fucking with the gravestones. He wasn't just the caretaker, after all. His parents and several friends were buried here. The last case of vandalism had been one he'd stopped himself. He didn't turn in the kids. Instead, Sam made sure they'd never try it again. Fear was a wonderful motivator and a few smashed fingers went a long way to changing a punk's perspective on the fine art of graveyard desecration.

Gethsemane was quiet, except for the chirping crickets. Sam stifled a yawn. He was about to go back for coffee when motion between two headstones caught his attention. He pulled his nightstick and shined the flashlight beam over the graves, dispelling the shadows. There was nothing there, but he knew he'd seen something.

"You have ten seconds to show yourselves, assholes, or somebody's going to be in for a world of hurt!"

The crickets fell silent.

Sam let the beam dance across the memorials. No trash or empty beer cans. No condoms. No signs that anyone had been fucking around.

And then the beam of light found darkness.

The shadows shifted, coiling like tendrils. One of them broke from the ground and rose up. It was human-shaped. The shadow stepped toward him. The flashlight beam disappeared into it. Gasping, Sam backed away. With a yelp, he tripped over a grave marker and sprawled in the wet grass. The flashlight rolled out of reach.

The shade rushed toward him. Sam opened his mouth to scream, and the darkness flowed into his mouth, filling him with coldness.

Sam closed his eyes.

When he opened them again, he was someone else.

FIVE

DANNY SHOWED UP early at Gustav's house. The old man answered the door, a cup of coffee clutched in one hand. His eyebrows furrowed.

"What are you doing here, boy?"

"I ditched school again. Something happened last night. I need to study more."

"Yes. Study is good. After school, you come here and study."

"Screw that. I want to study *now*."

"You must learn patience. That is important. Patience is one of the keys to magic. Go back to school and study there."

"Why? If I can do magic—why do I need school?"

Gustav's eyes glittered. Laughing, he sat the coffee mug down and swatted Danny across the back of his head. The blow was light, but sent Danny staggering.

"Hey," Danny shouted. "What'd you do that for?"

"Do you want to argue or do you want answer to question?"

"Answer my question. Why should I go to school?"

"Why? To know magic, you need to know the world. They are the same thing, boy. I told you before, you need knowledge. Magic is no good without knowledge."

Gustav picked up his coffee mug and Danny followed him inside. The old Russian collapsed into a sagging recliner. The springs groaned. The television droned in the background. Reagan was meeting with Gorbachev, and Bruce Springsteen had just announced a tour for *Born in the USA*. Gustav glanced at the TV and the sound muted. Then he turned his attention back to Danny.

"Something happened last night, yes?"

Danny nodded. "On my way home, I thought I heard something down by that old Greek restaurant that closed. You know where I mean?"

Gustav nodded. "Yes. I miss it. They had good food."

"Well, I was there. I...I got scared. I leaned against the building and closed my eyes and..."

Gustav leaned forward, his gaze intent.

"When I opened my eyes again, I was home. It's like I jumped or something."

"You opened a door, traveled through the Labyrinth. How did you do that?"

"I don't know." Danny shrugged. "I read a little about it last night, but I don't know how I did it."

"But I know, because I went to school."

"You're also a sorcerer."

"Nyet." Gustav shook his head. "I study and practice, even still. That is all. I never stop learning."

"Yeah, but you study here, not in school."

Gustav lit a cigarette and threw the pack to Danny. "I study everything. The more I know, the more I can do. That is how I join the Kwan."

"The what?"

Gustav shook his head. "Never mind. Is not important. What is important is that my knowledge makes my magic strong. Like shop class and geometry?"

"You lost me."

"Geometry. It is class in school, no?"

"How does frigging geometry help me with magic?"

"If you know geometry, you know how much space is in a box. If you know the space in the box, you can fill it."

Gustav handed him the lighter. Danny lit his cigarette, inhaled, and then passed the lighter and the cigarette pack back to him.

"Well," Danny said, "I can fill the box by pouring water in the opening."

Gustav scrunched up his face and imitated Danny's words. If it was supposed to be a perfect impersonation, it failed. Danny glared at him.

"You have a good brain, boy. Use it."

He opened the pack of cigarettes and dumped them out on the coffee table. Then he closed the pack again and handed it to Danny. "Here. How much does this hold?"

"Twenty cigarettes."

"Ah, yes, but how much water? How much gold?"

"It's not gonna hold water. It leaks. And who cares how much gold it holds? It's not like we have any."

Gustav snatched the empty pack from Danny's hands. He held it out in front of him and closed his eyes. He muttered something in Russian. Then he opened his eyes again and tossed it back Danny. The pack hit him in the chest. It shouldn't have hurt, but it did. Danny grunted as the box bounced off his thigh. He reached down and picked it up. It was heavy— no longer empty.

Slowly, Danny opened it and shook the contents into his palm. He stared at the dull yellow lump.

Gold.

"How? How the hell did you do that?"

Gustav tapped his head with one long finger. "I learned how. Magic is limited by knowledge. You have to know what you want and how to make it happen, yes? What is chemical composition of gold? Do you know? If not, you can make pretty colored rock instead of the real thing. Magic is a tool. Like a knife, or wheel. Is only as good as what you know."

Danny held the gold in his trembling hands. He didn't know how much gold went for per ounce, but he guessed he was holding that dirt bike in his hands—and then some. His heart rate increased. He licked his lips. While he stared at it, Gustav got up and went into the kitchen. He returned with a fresh cup of coffee and stubbed his cigarette out in an ashtray.

"Here." Gustav held out his hand.

Danny regretfully returned the gold. Then he glanced around the living room. The place was a dump.

"How come you live here, Gustav? I mean, if you can make gold, then you could live in any mansion you wanted. Why even live in Brackard's Point? You could be in a Manhattan penthouse."

"I like it here. I get a mansion then I have to make money all the time just to keep it up. Here, I have little house. I clean it myself and don't worry about money. I need more, I can always get it. Money is a tool, too. Just like magic."

"Yeah, but it's a nice tool to use."

"You are young. You do not understand." Gustav tapped the gold lump. "This can buy you things, but then you have to make more. Sooner or later, people ask questions you don't want to answer."

He handed the gold back to Danny.

"I can keep it?" Danny asked, surprised.

Gustav nodded. "Da, you keep. But, you also go to school instead of hunting crabs for money. Go to school because you need to learn, yes?"

That was all the convincing Danny needed. Already, he was figuring out how to cash in the gold and where he'd keep the money until he could get the dirt bike. No way could he let his mom find the cash. Not this time.

He paused in his thoughts.

"Gustav, can magic change people?"

"How do you mean?"

"Well, my mom. She's a drunk. Can I make her sober with magic?"

"For that, you need a *lot* of school. What part of her mind do you change? You make her not want alcohol and maybe she wants cocaine, instead. You make her not want anything then maybe she forgets to eat and starves. Your mother stays clean and maybe she wonders why you spend so much time with old Russian bum, yes? Nyet. The mind is dangerous to play with. Your brain must be strong first."

"But it can be done?"

"Why you think love spells work so good? Of course it can be done! But first, you must know the mind, or you make bad mistakes."

"Have you ever made a mistake?"

"Yes," Gustav whispered. "Many mistakes. Many sacrifices."

"Sacrifices? Like, what kind?"

"Is not important. What is important is that you go to school before truant officer finds you here. We would both have to explain, yes? And that wouldn't be good. Now go."

Weeks passed. Danny went back to school and studied hard. Soon, he forgot about the dirt bike and escaping Brackard's Point. He pushed those plans aside and focused on class instead. He begged off doing things with his friends and went to the library instead, a building he'd spent years actively avoiding. He discovered the sciences wing, with textbooks, dictionaries of medical terminology, and a copy of Grey's Anatomy. Gustav continued teaching him every other day. One day to listen, one day to think, was how the old Russian put it. First you learn, then you absorb.

At night, Danny thought about what he'd learned, and wondered how long before he could change Brackard's Point into a place he could tolerate.

Bedrik stayed busy, too. His army continued to grow with each trip to Gethsemane. Edward T. Rammel's shade dwelled inside Tony Amiratti Junior. Rammel was grateful for the second life, the chance to experience everything all over again—and to experience it as someone else. Since the senior Amiratti was in Atlantic City these days at the request of Marano, Tony controlled much of his father's local empire. Thus, Bedrik, who commanded Rammel's shade, was now in charge of the town's organized crime. It was the first step towards dominion.

Gethsemane's night watchman, Sam Oberman, had been his second recruit, taken over by the shade of a drunk driver named Thomas Church. With Oberman under his control, Bedrik could work in the cemetery without concern of getting caught. With each shade he freed from the grave, another of the town's most influential citizens became his pawn. Attorneys, bank managers, town officials, the fire chief, ministers, even the zoning officer; they were all puppets on his strings, all doing his bidding. Slowly, Michael Bedrik possessed Brackard's Point.

Of course, not all of the transitions were smooth. There were flaws in any plan. Bumps in the road. The unexpected discovery of Martin's body had been the first.

Erik Riley was the second.

Erik Riley had been a drug addict in life. Cocaine was his drug of choice, shooting up his method of delivery. He'd died of an overdose the night of his senior prom. He'd raged from beyond the grave about how unfair it had all been—until Bedrik summoned his shade.

"You've disappointed me," Bedrik whispered, squatting next to the body. "What should I do with you now?"

Erik looked up at his master through Chief Winters' eyes, and knew fear for the first time since his death.

Bedrik held his hands out; his palms hovered inches from the big man's heaving chest. Inside, he felt Erik's shade fighting to hold on.

"What to do," Bedrik wondered aloud. "What to do with you?"

Once inside the body of Chief Winters, Erik's shade had reverted to his old habits. Now he lay here on the floor of Chief Winters' home, a needle jutting from his arm, his skin the color of death. Having the chief of police die of a drug overdose wasn't part of Bedrik's new power scheme. A drug scandal would increase public scrutiny. He'd planned on infiltrating the media eventually, but not this soon. And not before news of Chief Winters' death would be plastered all over the papers and broadcasts, attracting unwanted attention to Brackard's Point.

But neither could he allow Erik's shade to continue inhabiting the policeman's body. Erik had proven himself unreliable; unable to avoid the sins of his past life.

Bedrik stood up. His knees popped, loud in the silence. He winked at Winters.

"Stay here. I'll be right back."

Erik whimpered through Winters' mouth.

Bedrik went into the kitchen and searched through the cupboards until he found a canister of salt. Then he returned to the living room and poured the salt out in a circle around the policeman's body.

"Erik Riley," he said, "I have bound you to me, and commanded you to do my bidding. It is through my power that your shade walks the earth again. Now, I command you to return to nothingness. I cast you out of this form, cast you out of this existence, and cast you out of this plane. Get thee behind me and do not return. Your shade shall fade with the dawn."

The circle of salt began to glow.

Chief Winters jerked upright, muscles still twitching from the overdose. Erik Riley's shade screamed inside him. Winters stumbled to his feet inside the circle. The needle fell from his arm. His eyes rolled into the back of his head. His heart, already weakened by his lifestyle and the excesses of the shade inhabiting him, ruptured. At the same time, his consciousness briefly returned. His eyes widened in recognition.

"Mr. Bedrik? What the hell?"

Then he toppled over, dead.

Bedrik didn't move. It wasn't over.

Erik Riley's spirit screamed again. Darkness oozed from the Chief's pores, mouth, and nostrils, and dripped from the corners of his eyes. It reformed briefly into a human shape. Then Bedrik stepped forward, took a deep breath, and blew. The shade, torn completely away from Winters' body, dissipated. Bedrik continued blowing. Inside the living room, the wind howled. The salt drifted into the air, swirling like snow. The scattered globules of shadow attached themselves to the minute grains and drifted through the open door, vanishing into the night.

Finally, Bedrik relaxed. The winds died down. Silence returned. In the hallway, the clock struck twelve.

The next morning, when he didn't show up for work and calls to his home went unanswered, Chief Winters would be found dead of a massive coronary. There would be no signs of a disturbance, nothing that would lead investigators to assume foul play had been involved. No trace of Michael Bedrik's presence would be found. Not even a grain of salt.

"Well," Bedrik muttered, stepping outside. "I suppose I'll need more policemen."

He'd consolidated his power, begun exerting his influence over the town, and taken care of the Erik Riley problem. Now it was time to learn the identity of the person who'd discovered Martin's body and find out how much they knew.

Six

SCHOOL WAS FINISHED for the day, but Danny remained behind, reading a book in the school library; *Magick in Theory and Practice* by Aleister Crowley. Danny had bought it at the used bookstore on Harbor Street. Gustav had scoffed, but then insisted that he read it anyway. "Crowley was insane," the Russian said, "but is important to gain knowledge even from the crazy, yes?"

"Danny?"

Mr. Bedrik's voice surprised him. Danny jumped. He'd been so engrossed in the book that he hadn't realized the man was there.

"Yeah?"

Mr. Bedrik was a hard-ass. Danny didn't like him; had often skipped his class the year before. But now, the teacher was looking at him with a different expression. Not contempt or disapproval, but one of impressed surprise.

"I didn't expect to see you here." The teacher sat down next to him in one of the empty chairs. "After school detention?"

"No," Danny mumbled. "Just reading."

"Crowley." Mr. Bedrik nodded toward the bookshelves. "The Master Therion. I can't imagine you found that in here."

Danny shook his head, and then closed the book.

"I have to admit, Danny. I'm impressed. That's awfully advanced reading for a boy your age, especially given your academic past. Is this some sort of heavy metal thing? What's that new band—Slayer, I believe? Do they use him in one of their songs?"

Danny shrugged. "No. I just thought it was interesting."

"Indeed?" Bedrik smiled. "And you like it?"

"So far."

"You should try *Aceldama*, his first published collection of poems. That was always my personal favorite."

Danny's eyes widened. "You read this stuff?"

Mr. Bedrik smiled. "Don't sound so surprised, Danny. A thirst for knowledge is a good thing. Crowley himself said that 'the solution is to develop consciousness so that we no longer think as a child or a school boy does' and are 'capable of comprehending incommensurables as pertinent to our own formula.' So yes, I've read him. I read everything, all subjects. I have a wide variety of interests."

"You...do you...practice it?"

"No. I just like to stay informed. You're never too old to learn more."

"You sound like Gustav," Danny said. A second later, he realized the slip and shut his mouth.

"You know Gustav?" Mr. Bedrik sounded surprised. "The old bum who hangs around downtown?"

"Yeah," Danny said. "A little. I mean, I've seen him around town. We're not friends or anything. You know him, too?"

"Oh yes. I am aware of him. And you should be careful around him. He's no good."

"He's okay," Danny said. "I mean, he's not a pervert or anything. His house is a dump, but he's nice. No job, but he's smart."

"How would you know? Didn't you just say that you're not friendly with him?"

"Well..." Danny paused, trying to think of a way to cover. For some reason, Mr. Bedrik's interest in Gustav made him uncomfortable. "We talk about books sometimes. That's all."

"Do you discuss Crowley with him?"

"N-no."

"Danny, lying does not become you."

"Yes. Sometimes I talk to him. Happy? But so what?"

"No reason." Mr. Bedrik stood up. "I have things to attend to. You really should go home, Danny. School is done for the day. It's nice outside. Do you really want to spend the evening reading books?"

"I thought Crowley said knowledge was a good thing?"

Mr. Bedrik's smile faded. "He also said 'A little knowledge is a dangerous thing; more than a little is certain disaster.' Keep that in mind in regards to your friend Gustav."

"You think he's dangerous?"

"I think you know more about him than you're pretending. And yet, I think you don't know enough."

"What do you mean? Is he like a Russian spy or something?"

Mr. Bedrik laughed. "Hardly. But there are a lot of things about him that simply aren't as they seem. His name, for instance."

"What's wrong with his name?"

"It's not Gustav."

He walked out of the library. The doors swung shut behind him. Danny frowned. The teacher had acted...different. No hollering. No angry incriminations. No disdain. It was like he'd actually been interested in what Danny was doing.

Weird. His comments about Gustav were even weirder—but understandable. After all, most of the adults in Brackard's Point thought the old man was a simple vagrant, living in that ramshackle house. They didn't know his secret. Still, Mr. Bedrik had seemed to know *something*.

Danny felt bad for being suspicious. Of course Mr. Bedrik was acting weird. His brother had recently been killed. Danny shuddered, remembering how the crabs had eaten the body. Mr. Bedrik was probably just impressed that Danny was reading. He'd tried talking to him—and Danny had responded with mistrust. He glanced out into the hallway, but the teacher was gone.

For a moment, he considered running after him and warning Mr. Bedrik about what Matt, Jeremy, Ronnie and Chuck had planned for him, but in the end, loyalty to his friends won out. He wasn't a rat. Fuck that noise.

One month ago, Mr. Bedrik had caught Jeremy, Ronnie, and Matt kicking the shit out of Terry Hampton after Terry refused to let Jeremy copy his test answers. Everyone else had the smarts to let Jeremy do whatever he wanted, but not Terry. He was new, and didn't know about Jeremy's low tolerance of people who didn't share.

The three boys had caught up with Terry behind the shop class. Chuck and Danny weren't with them at the time. If they had been, Matt probably wouldn't have been involved.

Matt had moved to Brackard's Point when they were in fourth grade, after bonds had already formed between Danny, Jeremy, Ronnie, and Chuck. Sometimes, Matt still acted like the new kid, eager to please his friends and gain their acceptance.

Jeremy could be mean, and sometimes his cruelty was infectious, like when they fed the Alka-Seltzer to the birds. Ronnie always went along with whatever Jeremy suggested. Chuck and Matt were more reserved. They usually sided with Danny's calmer influence.

But Danny and Chuck were playing the new Paperboy video game down at the pizza place on Congers Road that day, and Matt had joined in Ronnie and Jeremy's madness. Hearing Terry's cries, Mr. Bedrik caught them. All three got detention. It didn't matter to Jeremy or Ronnie, but Matt's old man hit the roof. He'd given Matt the worst beating of his life. Since then, Matt had been plotting to get even with the teacher.

Danny returned to his book, and tried to forget about everything else. His lips moved as he read. *"Let then the Adept extend his Will beyond the Circle..."*

Extend his will. He felt like he was ready, even though Gustav said he wasn't. But he'd been studying hard, and he was ready to try.

Things were going to be different at home.

After a few more minutes, the words started to blur together. The school librarian cleared her throat and then looked meaningfully at the clock. Danny closed the book and left, heading for Gustav's house.

Gustav handed him a package wrapped in tacky gold foil and tied with a silver bow.

"What is it?"

Gustav sat down in his dusty recliner and waved his hand. "It's a present, yes? You do good in school."

"A present?"

"Yes, boy, a present. Wrapped in paper. Surprise inside. Present."

Danny grinned, forgetting all about Mr. Bedrik. "Can I open it?"

"Da. Open it already."

Danny tore away the paper and stared at the small, red velvet box. There were no markings or store insignias on it. He opened the box. There were three items inside. An old Zippo lighter, meticulously polished, with a weird design etched into the side; a half moon, sun, serpent, and an eye.

He looked up at Gustav. "What do they mean?"

"They are Colleges of the Magus. The Moon is for thaumaturgy, the Sun for alchemy. The Snake is for sorcery, the Hand for Necromancy, the Eye for Divination, and the Dagger for Hemomancy."

Danny squinted. "But I don't see a hand or a dagger."

"No. You cannot see them yet. You are not ready."

"Not ready? I'm learning, damn it. That was the deal—I'd go back to school and study. So how can you say I'm not ready?"

Gustav laughed. "You think I give you new rules, yes?"

"Yeah."

"No. *You* give you the rules. I only teach you how to see them."

Danny sighed. "I know you're Russian, but I really wish you'd speak English."

Gustav tapped his temple and then his chest. "You know here and here when you are ready. Some things you are not ready to learn. Some things are too dangerous. Some your mind is not strong enough to see yet."

"Like necromancy? That's for making zombies, right? Voodoo."

Gustav shrugged. "Necromancy is dealing with the dead. Never a good thing to learn. Necessary, yes, but not good. You are alive. The dead are dead and should stay that way."

"Why?" Danny had already wondered about the dead more than once. Could he speak to the dead, talk to his father?

"The world is big, but the universe is bigger. There are things that do not like to be known. You learn something, you can't unlearn it. Once you know, you always know. Is dark. Come outside."

Gustav got up and walked into the kitchen. Danny followed. They went out into the back yard, and Gustav pointed at the sky.

"How many stars do you see?"

"Hundreds."

"Yes, hundreds. Thousands, perhaps? And more too, but you cannot see them. They are endless. Limitless, yes? So is magic. You begin to see? Because magic is individual, is different for each person. There is no limit to how much you can learn. You study, you get knowledge. You pay price, you get more power. Magic is knowledge and power. Knowledge you learn. Power comes from somewhere else. You borrow it."

"Like a sacrifice?"

"Da, sometimes. The elements. Or concentration. A debt in exchange for what you did. Perhaps part of your life or energy, or maybe your soul, yes? You pay enough, you can do anything. But sometimes magic wants more than you are willing to pay..."

Despite the warm night breeze, Danny shivered.

"You are cold?" Gustav asked. "Let's go back inside."

They returned to the living room. Danny picked up his present again as Gustav sat down.

"Thanks," Danny said.

"The lighter is special," Gustav said softly. "Keep it always. Do not lose it."

"I won't. What else is in here?"

"You have eyes. Look."

Next was a small, black leather-bound book. The pages were blank.

"What's this?" Danny asked. "A diary or something?"

He could hear Ronnie and Jeremy. If they found out he had a journal. They'd call him a fag. He didn't tell Gustav, didn't want to hurt his feelings.

"Diary?" Gustav roared with laughter, slapping his knees. "What are you, a Sissy-boy? Nyet, is not diary. Is Book of Shadows. *Your* Book of Shadows. There you write your spells. Magic that is just yours and no one else's. No one else will be able to read it. They cannot destroy it. Is indestructible. When you die…"

He trailed off suddenly.

"What?" Danny asked. "What about when I die? What happens then?"

"Nothing," Gustav said. He smiled, but his tone had changed. He seemed sad. "You are young. Live long time, yes?"

"Yeah," Danny paused, studying him carefully. "But you said something once before, about—"

"I am old man," Gustav interrupted. "Crazy commie bastard. Your words, yes? But true. I am old and I ramble. Say many things. Now, look in box. There is one more present."

The third item was a new pocket knife.

"It is untouched," Gustav said. "Open it carefully."

Danny inspected the blade. It looked sharp. He ran his finger along the edge and blood welled up.

"So…" He sucked his finger. "What next?"

Gustav didn't respond at first. He stared at Danny intensely.

"Next? Next, we begin the real lessons, yes? But tomorrow. Is late, now, and I am tired. Go home, come back tomorrow, and we begin."

"Thanks again for the presents, Gustav. They're really cool."

"You are welcome, Danny."

It surprised him, hearing Gustav refer to him by name. Usually, the old man referred to him as "boy". Danny felt a surge of warmth for his mentor. Over the last few weeks, he'd come to think of him as a friend. He'd spent more and more time with Gustav and less with Chuck, Matt, Ronnie and Jeremy. He suddenly felt guilty about that, and wondered what his friends were doing now.

Bedrik stepped out of the shower. Steam rose from his body and fogged the mirror. Candles burned on the sink, their soothing fragrance filling the bathroom. He closed his eyes and sighed. He was calm, relaxed. Ready to meditate. He planned on seeking out whoever had discovered his brother's body. It had to be someone with abilities like his. Not Gustav. He'd taken great care to mask his true nature from the old magus. Obviously, the Russian wasn't aware of Bedrik's plan. If he was, he'd have made a move by now. He hadn't and that was a relief. It meant that Bedrik didn't have to worry about attracting the attention of the Kwan. But if it wasn't Gustav who'd discovered Martin, then that meant there was a third magus in Brackard's Point. Danny? Impossible. The boy had latent talent. Anyone could see that. But reading Crowley after school did not make one an adept. However, Danny knew Gustav, and he'd obviously lied about their relationship earlier. Bedrik was sure of it. Could the old man be tutoring the boy? Was Danny his apprentice?

Bedrik's eyes suddenly snapped open. He was instantly alert.

Someone was outside.

Someone had penetrated the circle around his home—a barrier invisible to the human eye. There was no sound. No flashing lights or blaring alarm; nothing to alert the trespasser that their presence had been detected. But Bedrik knew. He felt it immediately.

Moving quickly to the bedroom, Bedrik took off his towel and put on black running shorts and a t-shirt. Then he slid on his running shoes. As he dressed, he listened for intruders, but the house was silent. Bedrik slipped out the back door and moved through the yard. He peeked around the side of the house.

Matt Adams was crouched over the open hood of Bedrik's car. He recognized the boy right away. Matt was one of Danny's friends. He hadn't grown up here with Danny, the way Jeremy, Chuck, and Ronnie had—but he'd been friends with them since moving to Brackard's Point.

He'd been meditating, seeking an answer to the question of Danny. Now, here was one of Danny's friends. The synchronicity was not lost on him.

Bedrik's smile was cold.

Matt glanced towards the house and then the street, making sure he wasn't observed. Then he turned his attention back to the engine. His hands were grimy.

Bedrik silently crept up behind him.

"Can I help you, Matthew?"

Shrieking, Matt jumped, smashing his head on the underside of the hood. Bedrik grabbed the back of his neck and pulled him away from the car. Matt was big for an eleven-year-old boy, but no match for the older man. He tried to break Bedrik's grip, but the teacher squeezed harder. Matt's other hand held a pair of wire cutters.

"Let go of me. I didn't do nothing!"

"We'll let the police decide that, Matthew." Bedrik glanced at the engine. The wires had been cut. "I'll bet your father will be very happy to learn how you're spending your spare time. Imagine his reaction when you're expelled from school."

"No!" Matt lashed out, driving the wire cutters into Bedrik's side. The point punched through his skin. Bedrik tossed him to the ground and felt his ribs. His fingers came away wet and red.

"You little shit."

Moaning, Matt struggled to rise. Bedrik kicked him in the crotch. The boy collapsed, choking.

"Forget the police. Forget your father. You drew blood. I'll deal with you myself."

"Please," Matt sobbed. "I didn't mean to do it. I was just pissed off."

"Who else knows you're here?" Bedrik demanded. "Chuck? Ronnie and Jeremy?"

Danny?

Bedrik's anger faded. An idea occurred to him. It was perfect.

"Nobody," Matt moaned. "I swear. I didn't tell no one. Chuck's at home fucking around with his bass Ronnie and Jeremy went up to Hook Mountain to get stoned. I don't know where Danny is. We haven't seen him much lately."

"You miss your friend, do you?"

Matt looked up at him and wiped his nose with the back of his hand. "Who...Danny?"

"Yes. You're resentful of the time he no longer spends with you?"

"Well, yeah...sort of."

"Then I'll make sure you see more of him. Stand up."

"Are you gonna kick me again?"

"No, I'm not going to kick you. I'm going to help you. Come inside."

Matt paused. "No way."

"Come inside or I'll call the police immediately and you can deal with your father's retribution when you get home."

Lowering his head, Matt followed the teacher inside the house. He limped, walking slowly and cradling his swollen testicles through his jeans. Bedrik closed the door behind them.

Then the screaming started. It continued for a very long time.

Later, Bedrik returned to Gethsemane Cemetery and stood in front of a headstone. Sam Oberman stood guard nearby, his body occupied by another. A ball of fireflies hovered over the grave. The name on the stone was Timothy Wells. His spirit was enraged, his mind like a hornet's nest, seething with images. A crowbar. Blood. Teeth. Violation. A used condom. A child's Halloween mask. Bedrik didn't know what it all meant, and didn't care. If he'd had more time, he'd have searched Wells' memories in detail. But he didn't. Timothy Wells longed for release. For revenge. That was enough.

"Come forth," Bedrik commanded.

Timothy Wells' shade slithered from the soil and knelt in front of its master.

Bedrik returned home and the shade followed. They went inside.

The screaming continued.

Then it stopped.

SEVEN

"**H**AVEN'T SEEN MUCH of you lately, man," Chuck said to Danny as they walked to school together. "What, you too good to hang out with us anymore?"

"Sorry," Danny apologized. He felt guilty for blowing off his friends from the Hill. But he couldn't explain it to them either. Ronnie and Jeremy would laugh. Chuck and Matt would think he'd gone crazy. "I've just been busy with stuff."

"Like what?"

Danny shrugged. "Just school. Studying. Shit like that."

"Studying?" Chuck frowned. "Since when?"

"I don't want to be stuck in this town forever. I can't play an instrument like you. I suck at sports. And my Mom sure ain't gonna put me through college. So I've got to start doing better in school."

"Who are you and what did you do with Danny?"

Snickering, Danny punched him in the arm. Chuck hit him back. Then the two boys laughed. It felt good.

"Man," Chuck said. "You *studying*...and I thought Matt was the only one acting weird."

"What do you mean?"

"If you hung out with us more lately, you'd know. Two nights ago, he went over to Mr. Bedrik's house. He was gonna cut the wires on his car, the way Jeremy showed us."

Danny's stomach fluttered. "Did he get caught?"

"No."

"Then what happened?"

"We don't know what happened. He showed up for school yesterday and he was all buddy-buddy with Bedrik. Ronnie gave him shit about it at lunch, and Matt said it was all just a misunderstanding. Said Bedrik was an okay guy and he forgave him for the whole detention thing."

"A misunderstanding? Matt's old man beat the shit out of him for that. I can't believe he let it drop."

"Well, he did. Like I said, he's been acting weird. There's other stuff, too. He's been eyeing the girls like fresh meat."

"Nothing weird about that."

"Yeah, but even the ugly ones. And he's talking to himself a lot. He's really fucked up. You should talk to him, Danny."

"Why me?"

Chuck sighed. "You know how Ronnie and Jeremy are. If Matt opens up to them, they'll just razz him. And he won't talk to me about whatever's going on. I already tried. Maybe he'll talk to you."

"Okay," Danny agreed. "I'll try."

Danny tried talking to Matt during fifth period, when they had English class together. Matt's attention was focused elsewhere.

"What's your problem?" Danny asked.

"Check her out," Matt said, nodding towards Valerie Hutchenson. "What's her name?"

Danny was confused. "Val? Dude, you've known her since first grade. Are you on drugs or something?"

"Val." Matt said it slowly. "She got a boyfriend?"

"She likes Ronnie. You know that."

He smiled. "She's got a ripe little body."

"Matt, you're acting like a real creep."

"Am I?"

"Yeah," Danny said. "You are. Jeremy wouldn't even act like this. What's wrong with you?"

Matt ignored the question. "What are you doing after school?"

"I don't know. Probably studying."

"Is that old Russian guy gonna help you?"

Danny held his breath. How had Matt found out about Gustav? And if he knew, did the other guys know, too? Chuck hadn't said anything about it earlier.

"Gustav?" Danny smirked. "Why would I be hanging out with him?"

"I don't know." Matt stared at Val. "You tell me."

The bell rang, and the teacher told them all to take their seats.

Danny shook his head. "I'll talk to you later, man."

Matt nodded, his eyes not leaving Val.

Danny took a seat next to Val at the front of the class. While the teacher handed out worksheets, Danny smiled at her. Val seemed wary.

"What's up with your friend?" she whispered.

"I don't know. Why? Something happen?"

She looked around and made sure the teacher wasn't listening. "He grabbed my ass in homeroom this morning."

"You didn't tell on him?"

Val rolled her eyes. "No, but if he gets anywhere near me again, I'm gonna break his balls."

Danny grinned. "I'll help."

Val put her hand on his forearm. Her touch was warm. "My hero."

Danny felt like he was floating. He tried to speak, but couldn't. Despite the giddy nervousness, he also felt guilty. It was no secret that Ronnie had the hots for Val, too, even though he wouldn't admit it and never pursued it. How would he react if he knew?

Val leaned closer. "Just tell Matt to knock it off, okay? He's seriously creeping me out."

"I will."

She broke contact as the teacher came down their aisle. Danny stared at the impressions her fingers had left behind on his arm. When he glanced back over at Val again, he blushed.

The feeling was a different kind of magic.

Danny was heading to study hall when he heard the screams. They were muffled, coming from the custodian's closet. He knew the closet well. The lock on the door was busted, and sometimes he'd sneak inside with his friends to smoke. Something thumped against the door, followed by another scream.

"No, goddamn it, STOP!"

It was a girl's voice. After a second, he recognized it.

Val.

The door rattled in its frame. Then he heard laughter.

Matt.

Danny flung the door open and gasped. Matt stared at him in surprise, teeth bared like an animal. His pants and underwear were around his ankles. He was perched atop Val.

One small breast poked out of her torn blouse. Her lip was bleeding, her left eye swollen, her cheeks glistening with tears.

"Hey man." Matt grinned. "You want some, too? I told you she was ripe. Come on in and shut the door."

"You motherfucker…"

Danny grabbed Matt's hair and yanked him forward. The other boy shouted, twisting in Danny's grip. Danny pulled him off Val and out into the hallway. Sobbing, Val pulled her blouse together. Danny threw Matt to the floor and hovered over him.

"What the hell is wrong with you?"

Matt stood and pulled his pants up. "Me? What the hell's wrong with *you*, Danny? Is hanging out with Gustav turning you into a queer?"

"He's not queer," Danny shouted. "He's my friend."

Matt grinned. "So you *are* hanging out with him, huh?"

Before Danny could respond, Val leapt out of the closet and knocked Matt to the floor again. His head cracked against the tiles. Shrieking, Val kicked him in the balls. The air rushed from Matt's lungs. He tried to curl into a ball as Val slapped him repeatedly.

"Hey, you kids!"

The Principal, Mr. Sarandos, charged down the hallway, shouting at them to break it up. He shoved Danny aside and pulled Val off of Matt.

Holding each of them by the arm, he herded Matt and Val toward the office. Val protested. Matt said nothing. Mr. Sarandos glanced back over his shoulder.

"You, too, Danny. My office. Now."

Danny followed, his head hung low.

When they reached the office, the receptionist looked up in alarm.

"Oh my," she gasped. "What happened?"

"Not now, Grace," the Principal said. "Hold my calls."

He steered the three kids into his office, made them sit down, and slammed the door behind him. The room was quiet, except for Val's sobs. Outside, Grace began typing again. Mr. Sarandos sat down behind his desk and glared at them. After a moment, he took a deep breath and asked, "What happened?"

All three began talking at once.

"She told me I could," Matt said.

Val held her ruined blouse together with one hand and choked back tears. "I told you to keep your hands off me."

The Principal looked at Danny. "What did you see?"

Danny glanced at Matt. They were friends. They stuck together. But what he'd done... Danny's stomach sank. He looked down at his shoes. His voice was very low.

"I heard Val screaming in the janitor's closet. I opened the door and..." He took a deep breath. "Matt was on top of her. He had his pants down. He was going to...rape her."

Danny glanced at his friend. Matt's expression remained neutral, almost like he didn't care. That was weird. Wasn't he afraid of what his father would do to him this time?

"Matt," the Principal said, "is this true?"

"He's lying, sir. Val was the one who led me into the closet. She wanted to make out."

Val burst into tears again. "That's not true! You tried to rape me…"

Mr. Sarandos picked up the telephone. He stared at Matt while he spoke. "Grace, please call the police." He glanced at Val, and his expression softened. "And we'll need paramedics, too. Who's free this period? Bedrik? Good. Please have him come down here, as well."

He hung up the phone and sighed.

Matt glared at Danny.

Danny shook his head, looked down at his hands, and tried not to cry.

"You stupid little shit."

Bedrik kept his voice low, his expression neutral. Sarandos and Danny were busy giving an account to the police. Val was with the paramedics. Since he had no classes this period, the Principal had asked Bedrik to watch Matt while they spoke to the police.

"I'm sorry," Timothy Wells said through Matt's mouth. "I couldn't help it. She was warm and it's cold where I was. It's been so long."

"Shut up." Bedrik leaned closer, whispering into Matt's ear. "You were warned to curb your old desires. I didn't set you free so that you could return to a lifestyle of rape and sadism. You were to find out if Danny was being tutored by Gustav. If he was, you were to let me know. That is all. And now you've fucked it up."

The office door opened and the police came out, followed by Principal Sarandos. Bedrik straightened up and did his best to look solemn. He caught a glimpse of Danny through the open door. The boy appeared distraught.

The policemen were both under Bedrik's control, their bodies inhabited by shades, but they kept up the appearance of normalcy. They handcuffed Matt and read him his rights. Then, while the faculty and students watched from the windows, they led him to the patrol car and put him in the back seat. Bedrik did not accompany them. He stayed inside the office and watched Danny.

Danny was too upset to notice.

When the final bell rang, Danny didn't stick around to use the school library. For the first time since his agreement with Gustav, he couldn't wait to get out of school. The halls echoed with the ghost of Val's screams.

The walk home had never seemed longer. It hurt to think. Hurt to feel. What good was magic when it couldn't change what had happened, or erase the memories from his mind? He'd never felt worse. He'd ratted on a friend, an unforgivable sin. But Matt's sin was greater. Matt wasn't just in trouble this time. This was more than detention or a beating from his old man. Matt was in deep shit. And Val— Danny thought about how he'd felt when she touched his arm. Somehow, that made what had happened to her seem even worse. He was disgusted with Matt for what he'd done, and disgusted with himself for the guilty arousal he'd felt when he saw Val's exposed breast.

He wished that magic could make the entire day just go away.

Ronnie, Chuck, and Jeremy caught up with him on Ghilcrest Road.

"What the fuck happened?" Ronnie demanded.

Danny studied his friends. Ronnie and Jeremy were coiled tight, ready to snap. Chuck was sullen.

"Chuck said Matt was acting weird. Well, you were right. He tried to rape Val."

"Jesus..." Chuck shook his head in disbelief.

"Damn," Jeremy snickered. "Didn't know he had it in him."

"And you stopped him?" Ronnie asked.

Danny nodded. "Yeah."

"Cool." Ronnie seemed relieved. "But if you stopped it, then why did the cops arrest him?"

"I just said, man. He tried to rape Val."

"She told on him?" Chuck asked.

Danny didn't respond. He stared at his feet.

"Dude," Jeremy muttered, stepping forward, "tell us she ratted him out. That's what happened, right?"

Danny shook his head. The three boys pressed closer, surrounding him.

"You didn't narc on him," Jeremy said. "No way. Fuck that noise."

"Yeah," Danny whispered, "I did."

"Jesus fucking Christ, Danny!"

"Well, what was I supposed to do, man? He tried to *rape* her. I wasn't going to lie for him."

"Why not?" Jeremy hollered. "He's one of us, man. You chose Val over Matt?"

Chuck ran his hand through his hair. "This is fucked up."

"Don't give me that," Danny said. "You guys would have done the same thing. Ronnie? You like Val. You would have told on Matt, too. In a heartbeat. Tell them."

Ronnie didn't respond. He stared at the ground. Chuck looked away. Jeremy spat at his feet and glared at Danny.

"You know what," Danny said. "Fuck you guys."

"Fuck you, too," Jeremy shouted.

Danny pushed past Ronnie and Chuck, turning his back on them and walking away. He tensed, waiting for Jeremy to swing, waiting for all three of them to jump him. They didn't. Somehow, that made it worse.

Danny wanted to turn around, but he resisted the urge. Instead he kept walking. He felt them staring at him, felt the silent incrimination. They thought he'd changed. He didn't hang out anymore. He'd told on Matt. In their eyes, he was somebody else. But he hadn't changed. He still felt like the same person. Only now, he was the same person without any friends.

Except for Gustav.

He just wished the old man had told him about magic's price before he paid it.

Eight

GUSTAV STOOD ON the sidewalk, watching the house as the sun went down. The shadows lengthened. The insects sang. Pedestrians and cars rushed past him, hurrying home for the evening. Nobody noticed him, because Gustav did not wish to be noticed. He simply observed—an unmoving, unblinking sentinel, probing with his mind and senses. He didn't approach, didn't cross the sidewalk and step into the yard. He couldn't. Bedrik had taken care to safeguard his home. There were wards and sigils and circles of protection, all invisible to the untrained eye.

In a way, Gustav begrudgingly admired Bedrik. The other magician's power was strong, and his influence over the town grew with each passing night. He'd been clever from the beginning, masking his abilities from Gustav, working his magic in secret. Gustav hadn't been aware of Michael Bedrik's true nature until the discovery of Martin Bedrik's body along the Hudson. He'd read the body, read the signs. He knew what was afoot. The casting off of one's own shadow to gain control of other shades; very serious magic, very bad. And while Bedrik grew more powerful, Gustav's strength remained the same. He couldn't challenge his opponent. Not yet. To confront him here where he was strongest would be suicide. Nor could he call upon others from the Kwan. They would not help. Brackard's Point was his ward. He was responsible for it, win or lose. Besides, the others were busy with their own trials and triumphs. This was his cross to bear.

He only hoped that Danny would be ready in time.

Gustav counted on his power.

Gustav gazed up at the sky. Dark clouds promised rain. The shadows deepened. He shivered in the cool spring breeze. For the first time in a long time, he thought of home—and of the Nerpa.

"Enough."

Snorting, he spat a wad of phlegm across the sidewalk, towards Bedrik's lawn. Energy crackled, easily mistakable for a humming power line to those unattuned. But Gustav was in tune.

No, he could not confront Bedrik. Not directly.

But he could say hello.

Bedrik hung up the phone. Through his control of the police department and the District Judge, he'd been able to get Matt/Timothy Wells released on his own recognizance. Bedrik had considered just having his puppets kill the boy en route to the police station; say he'd resisted arrest, grabbed one of their guns. But despite today's fiasco, Wells might still prove useful. Bedrik was beginning to suspect he was right about Danny being Gustav's apprentice. It may have been the boy who'd discovered Martin's body. If so, then he had to assume that Gustav was aware. And that meant he'd have to deal with them both much sooner than he'd planned. He'd always intended to go after Gustav after his control of the town was total. No matter how strong the old magus was, he couldn't defeat an entire army of shade-possessed townspeople. But now, Bedrik might have to deal with the man himself.

Before he could consider it further, he felt a twinge at the back of his consciousness. The circle had been breached again. Could it be Matt/Wells, come to grovel for forgiveness? As he moved to the window, he heard a dog barking. Bedrik looked outside. He couldn't see anything, but he felt it. A presence. The sidewalk and yard were empty. He continued staring, forcing his eyes to focus on nothing and everything at the same time. There, near the tree; a shifting in the air, a shimmering spot where the world didn't quite look right, even though nothing appeared wrong or out of place.

Across the street, Kyle Wilkes was walking his terrier. The dog suddenly crouched, tugging at its leash, and growled. It, too, was staring at the spot beneath the tree.

Bedrik watched the spot from the corner of his eye, refusing to focus on it. Slowly, the shape coalesced into human form. Old. Bent. Haggard.

Gustav.

The old Russian waved at Kyle, who angrily urged his dog on down the street. Slowly, Gustav turned back to the house and met Bedrik's gaze. Then he smiled.

Bedrik cursed. His hands gripped the curtains. His legs shook.

"That bastard..."

Every blade of grass in Michael Bedrik's front lawn had turned brown. The maple tree was wilting, the leaves falling from the sagging limbs.

Come out, Gustav's voice rang in his mind.

What do you want, old man?

I am neighborhood welcome wagon. I know you, Michael Bedrik.

Bedrik grinned. And I know you, Gustav, whose secret name is Partha.

Gustav was visibly startled. Bedrik's smile grew wider. The Russian hadn't expected him to know his magical name.

Come outside, Gustav thought. *Say hello, yes?*

You're a fool, Bedrik replied. Do you really think I'd breach the circle? If you wish to draw me out and challenge me, you'll have to do better than this transparent ploy. Really, I'm surprised—and disappointed. After all I've heard about you. I'd expect better than this.

Gustav didn't respond. The old man suddenly seemed distracted. Bedrik frowned, glancing again at his ruined yard.

When he looked up again, Gustav was gone.

"Damn," Bedrik swore. "I'll need to move faster."

His mother wasn't home. Danny wasn't surprised. He hadn't expected her to be. A quick check of the cupboard confirmed that they were out of booze. She was probably down at Giordano's liquor store, restocking. That was the only time she left the house, other than for work.

Danny fixed himself a peanut butter and jelly sandwich, but threw it away after two bites. He had no appetite. He turned on the television and watched a few minutes of *Sanford and Son* before turning it off again. He wasn't in the mood to laugh. Danny felt like dying; he wanted to crawl into bed, curl up into a ball, and just float away. He wished for his mother, wished she was there to give him a hug and tell him it would be okay.

But the only thing his mother hugged was the vodka bottles.

He bet the Giordano kids were getting hugged by their mother tonight.

Sometimes, he wished he could wipe Giordano's Happy Bottle Shop off the planet. Toss a Molotov cocktail through their window, like on *The A-Team,* and just burn the place down. But could he stop there? Sometimes, when he slept, Danny had dreams in which the entire world was on fire. The dreams ended differently, depending on when he woke up, but they always started the same—at Giordano's.

When she was sober, Danny's mom was quiet and depressed. When she'd been drinking, she was loud and angry—or stupefied. Regardless of her state of mind, she was never the mother he'd had when his dad was alive. His memories of a happy mom were rapidly fading, just like the memories of his father. Sometimes, he had to look at his father's picture to remember the contours of his face or the smell of his aftershave.

He looked at his mother's picture to remember her smile.

The tears surprised him, sudden in their ferocity. His body trembled. His breath caught in his throat. His chest hurt. Danny sat on the couch in his quiet, empty home and cried harder than he ever had before. He cried for his parents, and for his friends, and for himself.

And when it was over, Danny decided it was time to make things better. Magic affected change in the magician's reality. The easiest place to start was his mom.

Gustav had told him to study, so study he had; learning about alcoholism and the human brain, dependency and depression. Some of it didn't make much sense, but he thought he was ready for what had to be done. First, he had to get his mother over her dependency, change her programming. Next, he had to prevent her body from crashing as the alcohol left her system. She'd been a functional alcoholic for a long time now, and he knew the physical withdrawals would be bad. He'd read that some people actually died from the DTs. He couldn't let that happen to her.

Step one, relaxation. Preparing his mind and body were essential. He had to be calm and alert. Danny began some deep breathing exercises that Gustav had shown him, forcing his breaths to come in slow and deep and exhaling so that he completely cleared his lungs. When he was ready, he focused on his mother. There were a lot of things that could go wrong, if he didn't do this right. Visualization was the key to success. He had to visualize the alcoholism as a living, breathing entity dwelling within his mother, and then destroy it without affecting any other part of her mind. In changing their reality, he didn't want to change his mom; he just wanted her to be free from the booze. He wanted her to be happy again.

He kept his eyes shut and floated, his breathing shallow and rhythmic. Then, in the silence, he heard a whisper—the whip crack of a feather, the echo of a cat barking. It seemed to come from nowhere and everywhere. Danny's eyes blinked open and he sat up straight. The living room was dark and empty. He was alone.

But the sound continued.

It shifted, resembling the padding of paws. One second it was behind the couch. The next, it was beneath the recliner, and then perched atop the lamp, and finally all three at the same time. His head darted back and forth, trying to track it, but he still saw nothing. His heart hammered, and his ears rang. The sound changed again to the clicking of crab shells. Whatever it was, he'd heard it before—that night outside the abandoned Greek restaurant, when he'd teleported himself. The same day he'd discovered a dead body...

...and discovered magic.

The sound *solidified* and Danny felt a presence in the room. The air seemed heavy, the atmosphere electric. The lamp dimmed; then flickered out completely, plunging the living room into darkness.

Whimpering, Danny pulled his feet up onto the sofa.

Headlights flashed through the gap in the curtains. A car pulled into the driveway, his mother; the engine's sickly whine was as familiar as anything else in the house. At the same moment, the presence vanished. The lamp bulb brightened again, dispelling the darkness. The noises stopped. Whatever it had been, it was gone.

Outside, the car door slammed. He heard footsteps and the jangle of keys. His mother opened the trunk. Bags rustled and glass bottles clicked together. Then she slammed the trunk. Her footsteps headed up the driveway.

Pushing the fear from his mind, Danny focused on his breathing, forcing himself to calm down and relax. Visualize. Despite everything that had just happened, he looked remarkably tranquil on the sofa, eyelids half-closed, mouth open, pulse and breathing slowing. Only his eyes moved.

The keys jangled in the lock. A moment later, the front door opened, and his mother walked in.

"You're home," she mumbled. "What are you doing?"

Danny couldn't respond. Although he remained still, his eyes widened. The visualization had worked—maybe too well. The demon Alcohol clung to her back. It looked like a mutant monkey-mosquito hybrid. A proboscis fed directly into her brain. He knew that his mind had created this thing to symbolize her dependency, but it seemed so real. Its flesh wiggled as she shut the door behind her. Its glowing, insect-like eyes regarded him without blinking, a thousand facets of glossy red. He could even smell the creature—rotten and spoiled and sickly. Its thick-toed feet clutched her shoulders. Her hair was twisted in its stubby fingers.

"Danny?" His mother sat the bags down on the coffee table. The bottles clinked.

"Hey, Mom…"

He was suddenly overcome with doubt. What the hell was he doing? Was it possible to stop the thing crawling on his mother? Was it really just his mind's creation, a representation of her disease, or had he somehow made it real through magic?

His mother collapsed into the recliner, kicked off her shoes, and rummaged through the bags.

"God," she moaned. "What a day. I hate that fucking place. How was school?"

"Okay," he lied. "Boring."

Sighing, his mother pulled a bottle of vodka from the bag and twisted the cap. Then she took a drink.

"Mmm, that hits the spot. I needed this."

The creature cooed, shivering with pleasure. Danny squirmed. If his mother heard it, she gave no indication.

She looked at him and smiled weakly. Then she took another drink.

The energies he'd been gathering inside coalesced and Danny let them fly, imagining them as a blistering ball that scorched the air between them. He thrust out his hands. Blistering light erupted from his fingertips and struck the demon in the head, severing the spear-like proboscis. Red energy fizzled from the hollow tube like blood, and his mother gasped.

The demon roared; a thousand nails across a thousand chalkboards. Its flesh blackened, blistered and exploded. Flaming chunks splattered against the wall, and sludge pooled on the carpet. His mother was covered in gore. She took another swig from the bottle, stared at his trembling hands, his fingers pointed towards her, and frowned.

"What are you doing, Danny? You look like you're having a seizure."

Incredibly, the creature was still moving. Its burning remains leaped into the air, narrowly missing the ceiling, and landed on the carpet, a headless, twitching abomination. Danny reached out with his mind and caught it, gripping the monster with his will, crushing the wriggling thing in on itself, tearing through its body like termites through soft wood.

His mother called his name again. Gray-green demon blood dripped into her open mouth.

"Danny, what's wrong with you?"

The demon vanished, obliterated.

"Danny? Answer me. Are you okay?"

He blinked, then raised his head and smiled at her.

"I'm fine, Mom. Everything's going to be fine."

"Good. You know, sometimes I—"

She trailed off. Her jaw went slack. Her eyes drooped. Slowly, the vodka bottle slipped from her grasp and clattered to the floor. The liquid sloshed out onto the gore. His mother slumped over in the chair, unconscious.

"Mom!"

Danny leapt from the sofa and ran to her. Her mouth hung open. She was breathing, but just barely. With one trembling hand, he reached out and shook her. His mother did not respond.

"Mom?"

He squeezed her hand. It was cold.

"Mom, wake up!"

She did not answer, did not move.

Oh no. No no no no no...

His vision blurred. What had he done? He'd wanted to fix things, make them right. But despite all of his confidence and research, he wasn't a magician. He was just a stupid kid. At that moment, what he wanted more than anything was to be comforted by the nearly lifeless pile of flesh slumped in the chair.

"Mommy?"

Still no answer. Frantic, Danny called for someone else—called out with his mind.

Gustav, come quick. Please come quick. Something's wrong.

If the old Russian heard him, he did not answer.

Danny had never felt more alone.

Outside Danny's home, the presence hovered without form, without mass. Only its emotions had substance—thoughts, feelings, intelligence. Revenge. It longed to break free, to walk the world once more. Distraught, it felt itself fading, slipping away again. Its anguished cries were inaudible.

Then it was gone.

Gustav smiled, waiting for Bedrik's response. His point had been proven. He'd let the other magus know that he was aware of his presence. Now the challenge would begin. The next move was Bedrik's. Be it psychic or physical, he wouldn't attack right away. His opponent was under the mistaken impression that Gustav was actually stronger than he was. Bedrik would be wary of a direct assault. Gustav counted on that. He had to make sure that illusion remained, make sure Bedrik continued believing he was stronger. It was the only way to buy time, and Gustav needed that time to increase Danny's power.

And even then...

You're a fool, Bedrik ranted. Do you really think I'd breach the circle? If you wish to draw me out and challenge me, you'll have to do better than this transparent ploy. Really, I'm surprised—and disappointed. After all I've heard about you. I'd expect better than this.

Before Gustav could reply, Danny's summons slammed into his head.

Gustav, come quick. Please come quick. Something's wrong.

The boy's voice was panicked, on the verge of tears.

Cursing, Gustav ran into the night.

Gustav did not knock. He flung the door open and stepped into the house, out of breath and hair askew. His gaze swept past Danny and lingered on the boy's mother lying on the couch. He sniffed the air.

"I smell magic, yes?"

Lower lip quivering, Danny nodded.

"Have you moved her?"

Danny flinched at the anger in his mentor's voice. Gustav had called him 'boy' again, rather than 'Danny'. He fought back tears.

"I...I moved her from the chair to the sofa."

"Move aside."

Danny stepped out of the way, barely able to look the man in the eyes.

Gustav dropped down on his knees in front of the couch and checked her pulse and breathing. He lifted up one eyelid and stared. Then he let it drop shut again.

"What did you do, boy?"

"I didn't mean to. It was an accident. I was trying to help her."

"This is help?"

"It was an accident! You said all I needed was knowledge and power."

"And you have neither. You've learned nothing yet. And power—power should be saved until ready. Not tossed away like..." He nodded at the limp form.

Tears slid down Danny's cheeks. "Can you help her?"

The old man shook his head.

"Gustav," Danny begged, "please, can you help her?"

Gustav muttered in Russian and then stood up. "I don't know. Perhaps."

"What can I do to help?"

"What can you do? Leave. Get out. That is what you can do. I need silence to concentrate. Go see your friends."

"I can't. They're all mad at me."

"Then go to my house and read. But do not be here right now."

"Why?"

"I said leave," Gustav shouted, waving his hands. "Do not question. Always with the questions, you are. Go. Get out. I can't concentrate with you dancing around like circus bear. Go away. I call you when I know what we can do."

Nodding his head, Danny left the house. The night was miserable, dark and windy, threatening to rain. It suited his mood. He didn't bother getting his bike out of the garage. Filled with restless energy and no way to focus it, Danny walked. The sidewalk beneath his feet was the same, but seemed different than the day before. Everything had changed. He'd lost his friends, and possibly killed his mother. And for what? For magic? To make things better?

Was it so bad, his mom's drinking?

Yes, it was. It hadn't been once upon a time, right after his father's death. But over time, it festered like a wound; the alcohol infected her bloodstream, changing her. She'd been beautiful once, everything a mom was supposed to be. Now, her face was puffy and there were dark circles under her eyes that she hid beneath a layer of makeup when she went to work. At night, she passed out in front of the television, and only got up on time if he woke her.

All he'd wanted was his old mom back, his old life, to be happy. He'd wanted the fucking dirt bike his dad promised him and the

Yankees season tickets and dinners out almost every night and for his friends to have a shot at good things, too.

Now he had shit.

Danny's hands curled into fists. The energy built inside him. He could feel it pushing against his chest and skull. Then the rain came. Thunder boomed. A fat raindrop splattered against his head. Then another. More pelted the sidewalk. The trees rustled as the wind picked up. He looked up from the wet concrete and got his bearings. He was at a crossroads. Six blocks from school, six blocks from where his best friends had decided he was a traitor, and six blocks from the road leading to the Haverstraw Marina—where it had all begun. Six-six-six; Danny still had a lot to learn about numerology, but he knew that was a powerful number.

Then he glanced across the street and smiled without humor.

Giordano's Happy Bottle Shop.

Neon signs flashed in the window. The cardboard standee of a buxom blonde girl in a miniskirt and t-shirt stood inside the door, advertising the can of beer in her two-dimensional hand. He'd seen the girl before, a beautiful fantasy promising fun and maybe even a chance to lose his virginity if he'd only buy a twelve pack of the brand she offered with an eager smile. He knew the beer well. His mom drank it when she needed something lighter than tequila or vodka.

"Fuck you," Danny said to the cardboard girl and the window between them. Slowly, he took in the rest of the details of the Giordano's liquor store. The feverish energy rampaging through his system swelled.

He didn't think about it, just let it happen. There were two customers inside the store, and Mr. Giordano was behind the counter. Mr. Giordano, the man who was there for his kids, who took his family on vacations every year, and bought them anything they wanted and kept his promises. How much of that had his mother financed? How many times had she taken his cash and left her little I.O.U.s, all so she could afford another bottle?

Fists pressed against his sides, Danny closed his eyes and pushed. Then he opened his eyes again and watched.

The people inside the store disappeared. One moment they were there, and the next— they vanished, blinking out of existence in a single heartbeat. Simultaneously, every bottle inside the building exploded, spewing their contents across the floor and shelves. Shards of glass shredded the smiling cardboard girl. The store window shattered and broken glass rained down on the sidewalk. Danny pushed again and the air inside the building grew hot. The alcoholic fumes saturating the store burst into flame.

The last of the energy drained from him. Danny suddenly felt very tired. He stared at the store, his mouth hanging open. The fire raced through the building.

"Oh shit..."

He turned and quickly walked away, careful not to run and risk attracting attention to himself. It was hard to do. He had to resist the urge to flee. The falling rain increased, quickly soaking his clothing. Thunder boomed again. Behind him, the store exploded. Danny spun around, shielding his eyes with his hand as a massive ball of flame engulfed the store. His ears popped from the pressure. Fiery debris pelted the three cars in the parking lot. A station wagon was thrown into the air, rolling three times before it crashed into a dumpster. Superheated air slammed into him. Danny staggered. He smelled burning hair, and after a moment, realized it was his. The small, fine hairs on his arms were singed.

The sky opened up, and the rain poured hard and fast.

It did nothing to extinguish the inferno burning inside of him.

NINE

COME HOME, BOY.

Danny wandered the neighborhood until he received the summons, making sure to avoid the liquor store. He didn't want to be spotted at the scene. Although he was calmer, he felt cored out and hollow. His energies had drained away, and what remained wasn't enough to let him tie his shoes without getting winded. Despite his fatigue, as soon as Gustav called him, he started running.

The Russian stood in the living room. His expression was grim. The couch was empty.

"Is she all right?" Danny's knees felt like rubber.

"She will be. I think." Gustav sat down on the couch and patted the seat next to him. "What you did, Danny...that was dangerous. Stupid."

Nodding with reluctant agreement, Danny sat down next to him and forced back tears. He'd cried enough for one day.

"The mind is breakable," Gustav continued. "Very fragile. You almost killed your mother tonight, but I think I fix the problems."

"I just wanted...I wanted to make her better."

"Magic is like gun. It is tool to use, but is more than that. This is why you go to school, yes? To help you understand better what you do, so you don't hurt people. Magic is dangerous, because it can't be taken away."

"What do you mean?"

"You have a gun, and I can hide it from you. Take it away and lock it up. You have magic; I have to trust you to know how to use it wisely. Yes? And what you did here and at the liquor store—that is not wise."

Danny flinched. "How did you know?"

"Is on the news. I take care of your mother. Then wait for you. I get bored and turn on the TV. Liquor store explodes and three people inside are found in the water half a mile away. None of them know how they get there. But I know. And so do you."

"I didn't want to hurt anyone. I just..."

Gustav put an arm around Danny's shoulders and squeezed.

"So, now you know, yes? You don't play with minds. You don't play with people. Because sometimes you can't fix what you've done."

"But we can fix Mom, right?"

"Your mother sleeps now. She needs rest. Tomorrow, you call work for her and tell them she's sick. Maybe after that, she'll be better."

"Maybe?" That single word had never seemed so dire.

"Da, maybe. We won't know until she wakes up, but I think I do good work. I am a specialist. What I did to her will help."

"What *did* you do to her?"

"That is not important. What you did to her, Danny, was not good. That is important part and you have learned a lesson from it. But she'll be okay, I think."

They sat without speaking for a while. The only sound was the television, where the local late-night programming had been pre-empted by coverage of the liquor store explosion. There was nothing left but the foundation.

"I can't believe I did that." Danny stared at the screen.

Gustav rose, crossed the living room, and turned the television off. Then he turned on the lamp and sat back down. "Magic requires control. You fell against a wall and wound up here, along with your bike, because you were lucky. You burned a building and no one died, because you were smart. You made them go away. But you could have killed them anyway. You got lucky twice. But maybe not next time. Remember that. Magic has teeth."

"So, are you mad at me?"

Gustav shook his head. "Nyet. Not mad. Disappointed. You should have talked to me first."

Disappointed instead of angry. That didn't make Danny feel any better.

Gustav patted the couch cushion. "Is more comfortable than my bed at home. I will stay here tonight."

"What? Why?"

"You made a mess today. Someone will notice."

"You mean like the police?"

"No." Gustav walked to the window and pulled back the curtain. "There is another like us in this town. Your teacher. Michael Bedrik."

"Mr. Bedrik? He's like us?"

Gustav nodded.

"How long have you known?"

"Since the day I met you. When we saw his brother's body."

"Is he good or bad?"

Gustav shrugged. "There is no good or bad. Magic is what it is, power and knowledge. Sometimes is used for good, sometimes is used for bad. This time, I think he is using it as bad. Very bad."

"Why?"

"Because, I've heard the dead screaming. That is never a good thing. There are lights in the graveyard at night where no lights should be."

"So what do we do? I can't go to school if he's there."

"Yes," Gustav insisted. "You go to school, is important that you do. We must appear normal. And you must talk to him if he speaks to you. You must make him think you are not afraid. How you say—keeping up appearances? He knows about me. He does not know about you."

"Actually," Danny whispered, "he might."

"Actually? Speak clearly, boy. What has happened?"

"Damn it," Danny said. "I should have known. I forgot to tell you."

"What do you mean? You suspected this?"

"No." Danny explained the conversation he'd had with Bedrik in the school library, how the teacher had been familiar with Crowley and had recommended other works. His expression darkened as he admitted to Gustav that Bedrik had asked about him as well, and his connection to Danny.

"He said something weird, too. That Gustav wasn't your real name. I was gonna tell you, but when I got to your house, you gave me the presents and I forgot all about it. I'm really sorry."

Gustav let the curtains fall back into place. "Is okay, Danny. You are young. You get presents, you get excited. Is natural, no? Besides, it wouldn't have mattered. He knows my name and that gives him power. But he does not know everything."

"Like what?"

Gustav's voice was flat and emotionless. "He does not know what I am capable of. I am willing to make sacrifices."

Bedrik stood in an alleyway, staring at the smoldering wreckage of Giordano's Happy Bottle Shop. Beneath the rubble, the fires still burned despite the rain. The storm's fury had increased throughout the night. Rain fell in sheets, mercilessly blasting across houses, cars and trees. The gutters overflowed and the runoff swept through the streets, washing away debris. The cold water soaked through his clothing, dripped from his chin and nose, and plastered his hair to his head. But Bedrik felt no chill.

His hatred kept him warm.

Gustav had breached the wards he'd so carefully put in place around his home. Granted, the old man hadn't pushed through with the assault, but the very fact that he'd penetrated them rattled Bedrik. Still, Gustav had fled rather than provoke him further. The Russian was probing, testing Bedrik's power and strength. And if his distraction at the end proved anything, it was that their encounter had left Gustav drained. That was why the old man left—to recharge and recuperate. Gustav wasn't nearly as strong as he'd expected. Bedrik knew that he needed to press forward now, attack his rival while the man was still weakened. But not here—Brackard's Point was neutral ground. And it couldn't be at Gustav's domicile. That would be foolish, giving the old man an advantage. Nor could it occur in Bedrik's home. Gustav had probed his defenses and found them daunting. He would not return.

There was only one place such a confrontation could happen; Gethsemane Cemetery. There, Bedrik's power would be strongest, with hundreds of shades at his command, just waiting beneath the soil. In addition, he had his army of townspeople whose bodies already housed the dead. If he could somehow lure Gustav to the graveyard, disposing of him would be easy. The Russian couldn't possibly withstand such an assault. His power would wane in the face of it. Then, Gustav would be under his control.

Bedrik turned his attention back to the wreckage. It had been all over the news. That was what had brought him here. Not the explosion, but the fact that three survivors had found themselves floating in the Hudson, rather than burned to a crisp.

Magic.

But it was raw, unchanneled. The work of an amateur. This couldn't have been Gustav. This was someone else. Bedrik ignored the rain creeping down his back and concentrated on the ruins. He was not as adept with temporal magic as he'd like, but there had to be evidence he could use. All he needed was to catch the scent.

Investigators combed through the wreckage despite the downpour. None of them paid attention to Bedrik and he returned the favor. His eyes glazed over as he concentrated. There, beneath blackened bricks—a glimmer. He focused, finding a faint trace of the power that had caused this destruction. With that dying ember, he caught the psychic scent. The rest was easy. The magician, whoever it was, had shed residual energy as they left the scene, like a fizzling sparkler. Bedrik followed the trail back to its source.

Danny's house. And Gustav was inside as well.

So. There was his proof. The Russian had taken the boy as an apprentice. An adept. And thus, he'd left himself open to defeat. Bedrik knew Gustav's weakness.

Danny.

Now all he had to do was exploit it.

Bedrik summoned his minions, and then hurried home to prepare.

Normally, the sound of the rain drumming against the roof soothed him, but Danny couldn't fall asleep. He finally gave up and wandered into the living room, where Gustav lay sprawled across the couch, snoring lightly. Danny shivered. The old man slept with his eyes open. Danny moved on to his mother's bedroom and checked on her. She looked peaceful. She hadn't woken yet, but Gustav seemed positive that she'd recover.

Danny sighed. Only a few weeks ago he'd wanted to leave Brackard's Point and never come back. Now, looking down at his mother, he wanted to stay. But could he anymore? His Mom was hurt. Matt had been arrested and was probably in the juvenile detention center. Chuck, Ronny and Jeremy were pissed at him. He'd blown up a liquor store. And his teacher was a renegade magician. None of it made sense.

If magic was so great, why did he feel like such a loser? Cool new tricks, same old Danny.

Exhausted, but still unable to sleep, he lay down on the bed next to his mother and closed his eyes. The only sounds were the rain and her soft, low breathing.

Finally, he slept. His dreams were full of shadows.

TEN

HIS MOTHER WAS still asleep when he woke up. Danny tried again to rouse her, but she didn't respond. Sunlight streamed over her pale face. As he looked at her, fresh guilt overwhelmed him again.

Gustav was already awake. Danny heard the shower running, and Gustav's deep voice signing a song in Russian. Despite his guilt and sadness, Danny smiled. Singing in the shower didn't seem like Gustav's style. Next, Danny called his mother's job, explaining that she was throwing up and had a fever. Her supervisor didn't seem surprised. His mother called in sick a lot. As Danny hung up the phone, Gustav emerged from the bathroom.

"Good morning," he said. "Did you sleep?"

Danny shrugged. "A little."

"You need rest. It begins soon, I think."

"What's the plan?"

"Always with the questions. That time has passed. I said last night, we act like normal."

"But what if I see Mr. Bedrik? What am I supposed to do?"

"Do?" Gustav's voice was stern. "You do nothing. You smile and pretend. If he talks to you, you answer. But do not tell him anything you don't want him to know. Just make—how you say—small talk."

"What are you going to be doing?"

"I will prepare."

"But what about my Mom? We can't leave her here by herself all day."

"I stay and watch your mother. I can do both at same time. You go to school and act like everything is fine."

"Is it?"

"Da. Yes. Everything is fine." He waved his hand impatiently. "Now go get ready for school. I make your breakfast."

Danny was doubtful. "You can cook?"

"Of course I can cook," Gustav grumbled. "I am a good cook. You'll see."

Danny took a quick shower—cold, because Gustav had used all the hot water—and got dressed for school. As he pulled on his jeans, he smelled bacon. The aroma filled the house. He couldn't remember the last time he'd smelled it. His mouth watered, and he hurried into the kitchen, where Gustav handed him two fried eggs and bacon on white bread. Impressed, Danny inhaled the sandwich. When he was finished, he felt much better.

"You see?" Gustav asked as he scrubbed the frying pan. "You are full, yes? Feel better.

Good food. Good for brain and body. Keep you strong and recharge your power."

"I do feel better," Danny admitted. "Maybe everything will be okay."

If Gustav heard him, he didn't respond.

Dead people began arriving at Michael Bedrik's home shortly after nine that morning. Edward T. Rammel was the first to arrive, along with the body of Tony Amiratti Junior. Matt was next, the adult rapist inhabiting him now cowed and apologetic. With him was the possessed Sam Oberman, Gethsemane's watchman. Within minutes, several police officers and town officials—all housing shades—arrived, as well.

Bedrik gave them their orders. Then they dispersed.

The magus smiled. It was going to be a good day, and an even better night. And when the sun rose over Brackard's Point tomorrow morning, there would be no one left to challenge him. The town would belong to him, his own private empire.

Danny didn't see Mr. Bedrik when he got to school. After homeroom, he peeked into the teacher's classroom and learned that he had called in sick. A substitute was standing at the front of the class. Danny breathed a sigh of relief. He wouldn't have to encounter the magician after all.

The same couldn't be said of his friends, no matter how hard Danny tried. Chuck and Ronnie were in several of his classes. They glared at him like a traitor, and when he tried to talk to them, they ignored him. He saw Jeremy in the halls and had to walk away when Jeremy threatened to kick his ass. Val kept her distance too, and that confused him. He'd catch her from time to time looking in his direction, pouting, eyebrows lowered in either thought or anger. As soon as Danny met her gaze, she'd turn away.

He tried to ignore them all and simply get through the day. It wasn't easy.

At lunch, he sat alone and felt like dying.

Danny looked down at his lasagna. He toyed at it with his fork. He wasn't hungry, but Gustav had said it was important to build up his strength. He lifted the fork to his mouth but stopped as shadows suddenly blocked his light.

Chuck, Ronnie, and Jeremy looked down at him, their faces solemn.

"Matt's out," Ronnie said. "We saw him out behind shop class while we were smoking."

Danny put the fork down. "How can he be out already?"

Ronnie and Chuck didn't respond. Jeremy shrugged. They continued staring at him.

"Did he say anything?" Danny asked.

"He wants to see you after school," Ronnie said. "You're supposed to go to Gethsemane."

Danny shoveled limp pasta into his mouth and chewed slowly, looking from one friend to the other.

"Yeah, so you guys plan on helping him?"

Jeremy snorted. "Matt don't need any help. He's gonna fuck you up."

Danny shook his head and kept eating.

"What are you gonna do?" Chuck asked.

"Just go away. You guys want to take his side, that's cool. It doesn't matter and neither do you."

Ronnie and Jeremy glared at him. Chuck seemed confused and hurt. Danny didn't care.

Jeremy leaned down, placing his hands on either side of Danny's plate. "Matt said you're supposed to meet him in the graveyard. Unless you're chicken shit, that is. Are you?"

Danny stood up quickly and pushed Jeremy in the chest. Jeremy staggered backward. His fists curled.

"Go ahead," Danny challenged. "You want to fight? Then let's go."

He regretted saying it immediately. A fight with Jeremy would delay him from getting home and finding out how his mom was, or what Gustav had planned. He didn't have time for detention. He stared hard at Jeremy. There were a lot of things he wanted to say, a lot of things he wanted to do at that moment, but he refrained.

Rather than responding, Jeremy paled and took a step backward. Chuck and Ronnie's eyes widened.

"I'll let Matt kick your ass first," Jeremy said, but his words had no conviction. "Come on, you guys. Fuck this noise. Let's let the pussy eat his last meal."

They turned to leave, but Danny wasn't finished. Jeremy's words stung him. He felt the familiar energies building inside him, and forgot all about his mother and Gustav's warnings.

"If you see Matt, tell him to come find me." Smiling, Danny picked up his plate. "Fuck the cemetery. Let's do it right here. Tell him that *I'll* be waiting for *him*."

Gustav's eyes were closed, his breathing slow and shallow. He sat cross-legged on the floor, motionless except for his hands, which he folded through a series of motions—Earth, the god Set fighting; Air, which symbolized Shu supporting the sky; Water for Leviathan; Fire for the Teraphim; Spirit, the rending and closing of the veil; the cross for the One slain; the Pentagram for the One risen; Isis mourning, the Swastika, and finally, the Trident.

Music played softly in the background. Danny's mother had a small, battery-operated cassette deck, and Gustav had turned it on.

The soothing strains of Vivaldi filled the room. Gustav let the music envelop him. He felt strong. Ready. As long as Danny didn't waste any more power, things would go in their favor.

The music slowed, then faded and stopped.

Gustav's eyes snapped open. He got up and checked the cassette player.

The batteries were dead, their power drained.

Synchronicity?

Whatever it was, sign or coincidence, Gustav was suddenly afraid.

After the last bell rang, Danny filed outside with the rest of the students, losing himself in the center of the crowd. He walked slowly, his head turning from side to side, looking for Matt or for Chuck, Ronnie, and Jeremy. There was no sign of them.

He joined up with a dozen classmates going in the same direction as him. One by one, they turned down side streets or stopped at their individual homes, bidding goodbye to the others. Their numbers dwindled to six, then four. When the last of them turned up his driveway, Danny was left alone.

And Matt walked in front of him, emerging from an alley.

"Hey, Danny. How's it going?"

Matt stood sneering in the center of the sidewalk, hands on his hips. There was no sign of the others, and for that, Danny was silently relieved. Fighting Matt was bad enough. He didn't want to tangle with Chuck, Ronnie, and Jeremy as well. Not now. Not today.

"You were supposed to come to the cemetery," Matt said.

Shrugging, Danny dropped his New York Jets book bag to the pavement.

"Fuck the cemetery. Let's get this over with. You and me, right here and now." Danny took one step forward and balled up his fists.

Matt shook his head. He wasn't much bigger than Danny, but he didn't seem nervous or scared.

"Look, Danny, I don't know what's gotten into you, but this doesn't have to happen. I don't want to fight you."

"You don't want to fight?" Danny scowled. "Then what's the deal with telling the guys you wanted to meet me in Gethsemane? What's that all about?"

"I wanted you to come there so we could talk. Not fight."

"Yeah, right."

"I'm serious, Danny. Why would I want to fight you?"

"Why," Danny sputtered. "Maybe because I told on you? Because you got in trouble?"

Matt smiled. "That was all just a misunderstanding. Let's talk about it. I'm sure we can reach an agreement. Work things out. We're friends, Danny. We shouldn't let something like this come between us."

Danny frowned. Something was wrong. Different. Matt wasn't talking like himself. The voice was the same, but the words, the grammar—they belonged to an adult.

"Come up to the cemetery with me," Matt urged him.

"Why? Whatever you have to say, you can say it here."

"No," Matt said. "I want to show you something."

Danny lowered his fists and took a step backward. "No way. I don't know what's gotten into you, Matt, but just get the hell away from me. I'm not going anywhere with you."

"What's gotten into me?" Matt laughed. "You don't have any idea, little boy. None at all."

Danny's stomach clenched. "You're not really Matt are you?"

Sighing, Matt turned his back on him. Hesitant, Danny took a step forward, reaching for him. Suddenly, Matt whirled around and punched him in the face. Danny's lips burst. He stumbled backward, stunned, and collapsed to the pavement. Matt took full advantage of Danny's position and kicked him in the balls. Danny cried out, gagging from the pain.

"That hurts, doesn't it?" Matt aimed another kick, catching him in the thigh. "I know. I've been kicked there twice myself in the last three days."

Danny sucked air and tried to respond.

"I tried to do this the easy way," Matt said, looming over him. "But you had to be difficult. My Master wants you in the cemetery, and I'm going to haul you there if I have to."

Coughing, Danny rolled over and curled into a ball. Through teary eyes, he glanced around the street, hoping for an adult or passerby, but the sidewalks were deserted.

"You think you're something special, don't you? Just because you learned a few tricks from that old man, you think you can screw me over and get away with it?" Matt's grabbed Danny's hair and jerked his head up. "Think again. Nobody fucks with me! Nobody fucks with Tim Wells."

The name cut through Danny's pain. Tim Wells? Wasn't he the rapist who'd died a few years ago, gunned down by the cops when he wouldn't surrender? Timothy Wells had worn a Casper the Friendly Ghost mask while he committed those crimes. He'd even raped his wife. He was crazy.

This was crazy.

"Get up," Matt ordered, yanking Danny's hair. "Let's go. Don't make me carry you."

Grunting, Danny struggled to his feet. His lips pulsed and blood ran down his chin. His testicles felt like grapefruit.

"Is that who you are? Tim Wells?"

Matt grinned, tipping an imaginary hat. "Pleased to meet you. Hope you guess my name."

"How did you get inside my friend?"

"I was given a second chance. And you almost fucked it up for me. But now, now I'm going to fuck you up instead."

Danny shook his head. "I don't think so."

"What are you going to do about it?"

"You told me your name," Danny said. "Names have power, dumb ass. If you know something's name, the rest is easy."

Matt/Wells lunged at him, and Danny unleashed the energy inside him. The power left his body in a rush, a wave of energy that erupted from his fingers and struck the other boy in the chest. There were no pyrotechnics announcing the attack; merely thought and the action that followed. Danny focused, tried to visualize pulling the shade of Timothy Wells from Matt's body, and blasting it back to the grave.

But that wasn't what happened.

Matt screamed as his flesh blistered, turned gray and sloughed onto the sidewalk. His eyes dribbled down his face, his exposed bones blackened. He took a step forward and his charred ribcage snapped, spilling his insides with a wet, red splash. He fell apart, liquefying where he stood, decimated by gravity and his own violent convulsions. His bones cracked and splintered. The skeletal fragments turned to dust.

Danny stared in revulsion. His stomach heaved. He turned away and threw up all over his shoes. His vomit splattered into the puddle of gore. Something dark coalesced in the center of the remains—a dark, swirling form that grew in size and then erupted into the air. It was a shadow, a human shadow, and it screamed.

Then it was gone.

The street remained empty. There was no movement from the windows of the homes. The yards were deserted. Nobody had seen. That didn't make it better. Danny trembled, horrified at what he'd just done. Just like the liquor store, the destructive wave had flowed out of him, uncontrollable and overpowering. And now, one of his best friends was dead as a result. Because of him.

Because of magic.

No, he thought. That wasn't Matt. It was somebody else.

But was it really? Yes, Timothy Wells' shade had been inside of Matt, but where had Matt gone? Could his spirit—his consciousness—still have been trapped inside his own body, a prisoner? If so, then Danny was a murderer.

He stared at Matt's remains and willed his friend to come back. He balled his fists and pushed with his mind, wishing for it to be reversed. He visualized the puddle reconstructing itself, flowing and shaping into a body.

Let me take it back, please!

Instead, the thing that had been Matt dribbled down a storm drain.

Danny sobbed. Gustav had told him that magic had a price. He'd said that sometimes sacrifices had to be made.

But he hadn't told Danny that it would hurt so much—or that the cost would be so high.

Bedrik felt Timothy Wells die for the second time.

Cursing, he picked up the phone and dialed the police.

Edward T. Rammel watched the house through Tony Amiratti Junior's eyes. The old man and the woman were inside. There was no sign of the boy.

Edward had enjoyed his new life so far. Power, wealth, sex—what wasn't to like? He got to play a tough guy, just like the mobsters in the movies he'd loved when he was alive. It had been daunting at first, pretending to know people he'd never met and trying hard to fit in, to not give away that he wasn't who they thought he was, but he'd managed. Maybe the fear Tony Amiratti inspired in people had helped. But since taking possession of Tony's body, Edward had given them all new reasons to fear him.

A police car rolled slowly down the street. Edward grinned in satisfaction. The others were arriving right on schedule, eager as he was not to disappoint their Master. Bedrik was already angry over Wells' failure. If they screwed this up...he shuddered, unable to contemplate the ramifications.

The car pulled to a stop in front of the house and two men got out. They glanced in his direction, looking at the bushes where he was hiding, and then quickly turned away.

Careful, you morons, he thought. Don't let him know I'm here.

The others approached the house and Edward tensed, preparing himself.

"Showtime!"

Gustav felt their presence seconds before they knocked on the door; three men who were not men but something else.

He glanced at the bedroom. Danny's mother slept soundly. He'd checked on her throughout the day and was satisfied with her progress. Another twelve hours or so and she'd awake, fully recovered.

Moving quickly, he ducked into the kitchen and rubbed salt onto his hands, feeling the tiny grains scratch against his calluses.

The knock came again, insistent. Gustav crossed the room and opened the door. Two policemen stood on the porch. Their badges glinted in the late-afternoon light. Their uniforms were crisp and clean. The men were young, mid-thirties, and in strong physical shape. One of them wore a gold wedding band. The other had a neatly trimmed mustache. Their police car sat at the curb, washed and glinting in the evening sunlight. But despite appearances, Gustav knew the men were not police officers. Oh, they had been, once. But no longer. Something else was inside them now—some*one* else. The dead lived, walking the earth in borrowed bodies.

The policemen who were not policemen didn't smile.

He'd felt three presences, and wondered where the third had gone.

"Good afternoon, sir," said the first. His nametag read, 'STINE'. The other's nametag said, 'PUGLISI'.

Nodding, Gustav returned their frowns.

"How may I help you?"

Stine hooked his thumbs into his belt and hitched up his pants. "We had a noise complaint, sir. Care if we come inside and have a look?"

"Da, I care. I do not invite and you cannot cross."

"Police business, sir. We do have the legal right to search these premises if we have reason to believe—"

"A policeman could, yes," Gustav interrupted. "But you are not policemen. Nyet. You are not men at all. You are little shades, playing at being men. Is not Halloween, little spirits. Take off your costumes and return where you came from."

Puglisi reached for his sidearm and Stine took another step forward. With a speed that belied his age, Gustav's hand shot out. He grabbed Stine's arm and pulled with his mind. Stine jerked as if electrocuted. He opened his mouth to scream, but no sound came forth. Gustav's fingers dug into his flesh, squeezing. Darkness flowed from Stine's pores and orifices, forming into a shadow and hovering above the body.

Puglisi fumbled with his holster, obviously unused to it. Without releasing his grip on Stine, Gustav laughed at the other.

"Your master should have given you more time to get used to your new body. You're slow on the draw, 'pardner'. Not make good cowboy. Me, I watch many westerns. I will show you."

Gustav cocked his free hand like a pistol and pointed it at Puglisi. A bolt of energy erupted from his fingertip and hit the officer in the chest. Such an attack, launched by a more inexperienced magician, would have had much more explosive results. But under Gustav's control, the shade inside Puglisi flowed from his pores, mouth, and nose, just like the other had.

Both shades floated in the air, tethered to their hosts by a thin wisp of shadow. Then Gustav made a scissors motion with his hand and the shades screamed.

"I have bound thee," Gustav shouted. "Now I sever those ties. You thought to challenge me, no? I have defeated the Nerpa in the cold wastes of my home. I have spoken with the Siqqusim and wrestled with Belial and danced with Pan as the leaves change color. I have walked through fire and rain and the spaces in between. You have no power over me."

The shades began to dim.

"You will not return to your graves," Gustav continued. "Nyet. You will not go to next plane or the Labyrinth or anywhere else. Even the Void is not for you. No Heaven. No Hell. You are not even dust. You return to *nothing*."

As he spoke, the shades faded until there was nothing left. The soulless bodies collapsed on the front step like sacks of flour.

Gustav stared at the police car.

"Easy to deal with shades," he grumbled. "Harder to make car and bodies vanish."

He stepped out onto the porch and dragged the lifeless officers inside. Then he straightened up, wincing at the pain in his back.

"Now," he muttered, "where did third one go?"

He no longer sensed the third's presence. Could he have been mistaken initially? Could there have only been the two? He hurried to the bedroom to check on Danny's mother. When he opened the door he cursed.

Danny's mother was gone.

The bedroom window was open. The curtains fluttered gently in the breeze. The sheets on the empty bed still held her body's impression. He could still smell her perfume— the only lingering trace that she'd been there. Gustav ran to the window and looked outside. There was no sign of anyone. He closed his eyes and reached out with his mind, but felt no presence. Whoever had abducted her—if indeed she'd been abducted—was already gone. How could he have been so stupid? The policemen were only a distraction, keeping him occupied while Bedrik got his real target. But why was Bedrik interested in Danny's mother? Gustav opened his eyes and turned back to the bed.

I have her, old man.

The voice inside his head belonged to Michael Bedrik.

Why, Gustav asked. She is not part of this.

Perhaps, but the boy most certainly is. And if either of you want to see her alive again, you'll both be at the Gethsemane Cemetery at midnight. Don't dally. Don't be late. And come alone. Just the two of you. No one else. If I learn that you've informed anyone else, especially your precious Kwan, death will be the least of her worries. Every Hell I know I will make her suffer. Do I make myself clear?

Gustav didn't bother to answer. Instead, he snapped off the telepathic link as easily as turning off an appliance. A slow smile spread across his face. Bedrik wanted Danny to accompany him to the graveyard.

That was perfect.

Gustav turned his attention back to the two dead bodies and the abandoned police car, intent on cleaning up all loose ends. He'd have to use magic, reluctant as he was to do so. It was the only way to make them disappear quickly and safely. Doing so would leave him taxed for tonight's confrontation, but that was okay.

He knew where he could get more power.

The house felt wrong. That was the first thing Danny noticed when he burst through the door. His mother's car was still in the driveway, but there was no sign of her or Gustav. The television blared to an empty living room. Phil Donahue was arguing with people who didn't believe in paying child support. Danny switched the channel to *The Transformers* without even thinking about it, and then turned the volume down.

"Gustav?" he called. "Mom?"

There was no response. The furniture was all in place, the shades drawn, just as he'd left it that morning, but something still seemed...*off*.

He checked the bathroom, but the door was wide open and there was nobody inside. Trying to ignore the feeling of dread building inside of him, Danny made his way down the hall to his mother's bedroom. It was empty. The window was open. Gnats buzzed into the room. He called out again, louder this time, but got no answer. Outside, the breeze shifted, making the curtains around the open window rustle. Danny sniffed the air. He smelled something pungent burning in the back yard. The barbeque grill? No, that didn't make sense. After a moment, he realized what it was—burning hair.

He ran back down the hall, stepped through the sliding glass doors in the kitchen, and darted out onto the patio. Gustav was stooped over the grill, his back to Danny. He was muttering something under his breath, a phrase or spell, not in English or Russian but a language Danny had never heard before. The barbeque grill's lid was closed, but thick, black smoke and flickers of orange flame shot out from beneath it. Danny's eyes watered. Here was the source of the stench.

Gustav did not turn around. "One second, boy. Am almost finished."

"What are you doing? Where's my Mom? What's burning in the—"

Gustav did not turn around. Instead of responding, He merely held up a hand for silence.

Danny did his best to stay quiet. He moved away from the choking smoke and staggered out into the yard. He saw no sign of his mother. The yard was full of weeds and trash. A leaning, sun-bleached fence separated their property from the alley. As Danny glanced around, he noticed something odd in the alley. There was one spot immediately behind his home where his vision grew blurry. He turned his head back and forth. Every time his eyes came to rest on that one place, his vision went out of focus. He'd read about this effect at Gustav's, had experienced it first hand when he'd discovered Martin Bedrik's body along the Hudson—even though he hadn't known it at the time. Hiding in plain sight—Oriental magic, more a trick of the mind than anything else. Ninjas used it, and Danny thought ninjas were cool, especially Snake Eyes on *G.I. Joe*. That's why he'd remembered it. He also remembered how to overcome it.

He stared directly at the blurred area and let his eyes un-focus. It was harder than the book had made it sound. He kept going cross-eyed in the attempt. Behind him, Gustav continued chanting softly, ignoring him. Danny tried again, seeing everything and nothing. His vision blurred again and then—

—swam into focus. The hidden object appeared.

A Brackard's Point police car.

"Hey, Gustav, did you know there's a—"

"Nyet," the old man barked. "Ten more seconds."

Danny sighed in frustration, and held his tongue.

Finally, Gustav turned around to face him. The old man tried to smile, but faltered. The smoke and flames inside the grill died down, but the stench still filled the air. Danny stared at the grill, and then his mentor. He gasped, noticing that Gustav's hands were bloody. The old man picked up a roll of paper towels and a bottle of degreaser that had been left beside the grill and proceeded to clean them. As he scrubbed his hands, he looked up at Danny.

"Now, you had questions, yes?"

"You're damn right I have questions. One, where's my Mom? Two, is that blood on your hands? Three, what's in the grill? Dinner? Because if it is; then it smells horrible. Four, do you realize there's a cop car back there?"

"Yes." Gustav nodded his head. "Yes, yes, and yes. Your mother is not here. Yes, this is blood. No, is not dinner on grill. Is very old magic. Make fire hot enough to burn meat and bone and teeth to ash very, very quickly. I think you do not want to eat what I'm cooking. And yes, that is a police car. It is our ride later on tonight."

Danny barely heard any of it. "What do you mean she's not here? *Where's my Mom?*"

Gustav lifted the hot barbeque lid and dropped the bloody paper towels inside it. Danny saw a mound of ash inside, and wondered what it was. Then Gustav closed the lid and stepped towards Danny. His expression was solemn, and when he answered, his voice was low and mournful.

"Bedrik has her."

Danny tried to speak, and couldn't. The yard seemed to spin. Swooning, he reached out and grabbed the fence to steady himself. When Gustav spoke again, the old man's voice sounded like he was far away.

"He sent his shades. I fought two of them. A third took your mother. But I know where she is, yes? We will get her back. Will get him, too."

Danny shook his head. His ears rang and his knees felt weak.

"You said you'd protect her..."

"I did." Gustav's tone was sad. "And I am sorry, Danny. I did my best. But it was three against one, and I am an old man. I think I do good, despite the odds."

"Do good?" Danny let go of the fence and lurched unsteadily towards him. "Good? That crazy fucker kidnapped my mother. How did you do good?"

"I dispatched two of his shades. Bedrik looses power, yes? And I know where he has taken her. To the cemetery. We will meet him there. We will finish this, and rescue your mother."

"How? If you weren't strong enough to take on three shades at once, then how are we going to fight him? He'll probably have a whole army up there with him."

Gustav stroked his beard. "He may. But I have tricks up my sleeve, too. And I have you. We go together, yes?"

Danny nodded.

"But first," Gustav turned back to the house, "we rest. You expended power on the way here. I know. I felt it. I did, too. Both of us rest and then we go."

"Rest? We've got to go now!"

"No. Midnight. Those are his terms. He has chosen the location and the time. We must adhere. If we go before, he might hurt your mother. We need to be strong first. And I still need to finish cleaning up, yes?"

Danny stared at the old Russian's hands. "Looks like you got all the blood off."

"Yes," Gustav agreed. Then he bent over and rummaged through a plastic garbage bag. He held up two police uniforms, along with underwear and socks. "But have not taken care of these yet."

"Where did you get—never mind. I don't want to know."

"Da, you do not."

Shaking his head, Danny went back inside the house and tried to rest. He didn't think midnight would ever arrive.

But it did.

Before they left, Gustav slipped a salt shaker into his pocket and insisted that Danny do the same. He did not explain why.

They climbed into the abandoned police car. Gustav drove. Danny stared out the window and watched the town pass by. He thought of Ronnie and Jeremy. Chuck and Matt. Val and the other kids at school. His friends from the Hill. The assholes from Snowdrop. Everyone in between. He thought of his mother, and of his father, and wished that his Dad was here now. But he wasn't. In the end, this place had killed him. Now it would probably kill Danny, too. He'd always hated Brackard's Point. Had always wanted to leave. For all he knew, he might very well be doing just that tonight. Leaving. There were no guarantees that they'd return from Gethsemane. This could be his last look. Danny shivered, afraid. Gustav turned on the heater. Hot air blew gently across their feet.

They drove in silence. Soon, Danny felt better. He reminded himself that with Gustav at his side, there wasn't anything to be afraid of. Gustav was his friend. Gustav cared. Gustav would protect him and his mother—protect them all.

"Everything's going to be okay, right?"

"Da. You will see. Everything will be just fine. Soon, we all be back to normal."

A few minutes later, after they'd grown quiet again, Gustav glanced over at Danny and gave him a reassuring smile. Then he looked into the rearview mirror. He kept his expression neutral, careful not to give anything away. The road and the town were lost beneath a sea of black. The darkness was following them, flowing after the car like a wave, just as he'd hoped it would.

The darkness wore the face of a dead man.

Eleven

BEDRIK KNELT IN the center of the graveyard, carefully scrawling marks into the ground at his feet. He took caution to make sure that they were correct, every nuance and curve, every line and squiggle. He disliked this part, using his hands. He much preferred to have his minions do the grunt work. He favored magic through concentration, cause and effect through mental strength rather than physical. But sometimes, a magus had to get their hands dirty—or bloody. Or both. Like cutting up sweet Dana in his basement; or what he was doing now—scratching symbols of protection into the soil.

The sky promised more rain. Thick clouds covered the moon. He'd need light for what was about to occur, so he'd once again summoned the lightning bugs—calling them in from far away. Had there been any pedestrians on the street, and they happened to look towards Gethsemane, they'd have thought it was snowing insects. Thousands of fireflies descended on the cemetery, blanketing the treetops with their mass. Now, dazzling balls of luminous green-yellow light hovered over the graves.

Finished with the last symbol, Bedrik stood. He brushed the dirt from his hands and looked at the designs, nodding with satisfaction. Only three people in town would be able to see them—him, and the two who were on their way. Bedrik raised his head, feeling the breeze. He felt them drawing nearer. Felt the boy's anger and the old man's apprehension.

He turned to his subordinates, the former Sam Oberman and Tony Amiratti Junior. They stood next to an old, moss-covered crypt, the white stone graying with age and pitted from exposure to the elements. The boy's mother was tied to the stone with black silk ropes. The silk was a crucial element—a requirement, as was its color. She was naked, her mouth gagged, eyes blindfolded with another swath of silk.

"Mr. Rammel," he said to Amiratti, "when they arrive, you will stand by the woman. You will not act unless I command you to, and then you will act swiftly. If I tell you to do it, you will pick up that onyx blade and cut her throat."

"Got it," Edward replied. "You want I should call some of Amiratti's men and have them on standby, too?"

"No need," Bedrik said. "However, have you noticed that your speech patterns are becoming more and more like Tony's?"

Rammel shrugged. "I've been practicing."

"Very good."

"What about me, master?" Oberman stepped forward. "What will I be doing?"

"You, my friend, will play a very important role. Come here. I'll whisper it to you."

The possessed night watchman walked towards him. Bedrik pulled him close. As Oberman leaned in, Bedrik flattened his fingers and hand like a knife blade and thrust it into the man's chest. Fingertips parted flesh like butter, cleaving bone and muscle and ripping through the soft organs inside. The shade inside Oberman—Thomas Church, the drunk driver—screamed as it oozed out of the shredded corpse. Bedrik sucked the spirit into himself, breathing it in through his mouth and nose like it was fog.

He wiped his bloodied hand on the wet grass and sighed with satisfaction. Then he looked at Rammel and grinned.

"I needed that. I'm tired. It's been a very long day."

"Couldn't you have just had a cup of coffee?"

Bedrik laughed. "Indeed. The effect is quite similar."

"Won't you need Oberman to keep people away from the cemetery?"

Bedrik shook his head, gazing down the hill at the sleeping town. "No more. After tonight,

I'll be done with the cemetery. All those names I recited earlier? Those are the remaining inhabitants. Every soul that is buried here. I've summoned them all. They merely await Gustav's arrival, as do we."

Rammel pointed to the entrance. Car headlights bloomed in the distance.

"Doesn't look like we'll have to wait much longer."

"Good," Bedrik said. "Now remember, stay beside the woman. And most importantly, whatever you do, don't break the circle. Your shade can traverse it, but if your physical form breaks it—even an inch, even just your toe—we will lose this game."

"No sweat," Rammel said. "I got it."

"Do not forget who you're speaking to, Edward. You may inhabit the body of that Mafioso, but I know your true name. I can send you back at any time. Show a little respect."

"I'm sorry," Rammel groveled. "Seriously, Master. I'm really sorry. Please forgive me."

Bedrik smiled. How quickly the dead man returned to his own mannerisms, rather than those of his assumed identity.

They fell silent and waited.

Gustav stopped the police car and turned the engine off. His hands hovered over the steering wheel, and for a moment, Danny thought he saw them shaking. Then the old man sat up straight and pulled the keys out of the ignition. He smiled and gently patted Danny's leg.

"Let us go."

"Shouldn't we wipe off our fingerprints or something?"

"Nyet. When we are finished here, we will take care of car."

"But..."

Gustav looked at him expectantly. "But what?"

"But what if we don't make it back."

Gustav shrugged. "Then it doesn't matter if they find our fingerprints, no?"

He opened the door and got out of the car. After a moment, Danny followed. The graveyard was silent. No owls or birds, not even a whippoorwill. Even the wind had ceased. Overhead, the sky threatened rain, yet no showers fell. No lightning flashed, and the moon was a dull, silver halo. Despite this, there was light—too much light. Gethsemane glowed with will-o-wisps. Hundreds of phosphorescent balls floated over the graves, turning night to day.

"What are they?" Danny whispered.

"Ghost lanterns," Gustav said. "Bugs."

"Gross."

"Yes. But he needs them."

"For what?"

"The shades of the dead, they are like shadows. They need light. He is making sure they have it."

They started down the path. Gustav warned Danny to stay behind him at all times, and to not speak to Bedrik, even if the man spoke to him. "Say nothing. Only watch."

"But how am I gonna help if I'm just watching?"

"You will help. You will see."

"What about my Mom?"

"He will have her protected in circle. Cannot break the boundaries. Do not approach her, no matter what. Not until I say. You do, and she will die. You understand, yes? Like in the books?"

Danny nodded.

"Good."

Gustav pulled the salt shaker from his pocket and sprinkled some on his hands. He had Danny do the same, and then advised him to save the rest.

They continued down the path, passing tombstones on each side of them. Gustav glanced over his shoulder once, but when Danny looked behind them, all he saw was darkness. Even the police car was gone now, swallowed up by the night.

He was familiar with Gethsemane. He'd goofed around here before with Ronnie, Chuck, Jeremy and Matt—sharing an Old Milwaukee they'd stolen from one of the older kids or smoking cigarettes and looking at the stars. But somehow, it all seemed different now. There was nothing reassuring or familiar.

Shadows loomed everywhere, and when he looked straight ahead, Danny was sure he saw them moving out of the corner of his eye. When he'd look, they stopped.

"No," Gustav muttered. "Your eyes do not deceive you. The dead have come out to welcome us."

"Can they..." Danny swallowed. "Will they attack?"

"Nyet. Not yet. They will wait."

"For what?"

Gustav pointed. "For him."

Ahead of them was Mr. Bedrik, dressed as if for school in a dark suit and tie, and a long, executive-style overcoat. Another man stood near him, someone Danny didn't recognize. But he recognized the woman lying next to the man. His eyes widened. He stopped walking and curled his fists.

"Mom!"

"Stop," Gustav hissed. "Remember what I said. Is important. You say nothing, do nothing. Must control your power, not waste it."

"Fuck that."

Danny didn't walk towards the teacher. He stormed. With every step he took, the anger inside of him grew brighter, a smoldering ember that soon blazed as bright as the lightning bugs all around them. Gustav reached for him, but Danny was quicker. Energy leaked from him, marking his path. Each footstep wilted the grass overtop the graves, or weakened the asphalt path as if a giant had stepped there. The leaves fell from the trees.

"Boy," Gustav yelled, "Get back here. You must conserve your power."

Ignoring him, Danny continued on his way, feeling the power swell inside of him with each step. His rage grew hotter, more focused with every breath he took. The sight of his mother lying naked and helpless on a stone crypt, the memories of Matt exploding, of the look in Val's eyes—all of it was fuel for the fire. His fury was a blind, living thing inside of him, a monstrous, cancerous creature that knew no boundaries.

"Hello, Danny," Bedrik called, his tone friendly. "You're out awfully late for a school night." he looked over the boy's shoulder. "Gustav, you really should be more prudent with your young apprentice."

Danny didn't respond. Not because he remembered Gustav's instructions, but because his rage had muted him. He stepped closer and saw a white circle of powder surrounding Bedrik, the other man, and his mother. Mystic sigils glowed in the firefly light. More lines were written into the trees, and the headstones that surrounded them. He noticed something else, too—and it filled him with dread. Danny knew where they were. He recognized this portion of the cemetery. Recognized the tombstone Mr. Bedrik was leaning against.

It was his father's grave.

"Yes, Danny." Bedrik smiled. "It's a family reunion. You. Your mother. And even your dear, sweet, departed daddy. Come say hello."

"Enough." Gustav pushed past Danny and approached the edge of the circle. "Boy is not part of this. It is you and me, Bedrik."

Bedrik laughed. "Oh, Gustav, you've watched too many American movies. Who do you think you are, Chuck Norris? Clint Eastwood? The boy is a part of this. His family, too. They all are." He gestured towards the town. "All of them, every man, woman and child, alive or dead. They belong to me."

"Nyet. I will not allow it."

"You have no choice."

While the two men faced off, the energies inside Danny built to a crescendo. He closed his eyes and pushed, visualizing Mr. Bedrik flying backwards through the air, as if he'd been struck by a giant, invisible hand. The magic leapt from his body and raced towards the teacher.

"No," Gustav cried.

Bedrik did not move. He simply smiled.

The wave reached the circle, crashed against the barrier and flowed back to its source, knocking Danny to the ground. When he was younger, Danny had once licked a nine volt battery on a dare from Chuck. He remembered how the charge had tingled his tongue. That was his only run-in with an electrical shock until now. The sensation that now coursed through his body was like that, but a thousand times worse. It felt like ants were crawling under his skin and spreading through his muscles, eating everything inside of him as they advanced. He tried to scream but nothing came out. He struggled to his feet, and glanced at Gustav. The old man was chanting something. His eyes had rolled up into the back of his head.

"Stay," Bedrik whispered, making a motion with his hand.

Danny tried to step towards Gustav and found that he couldn't. He grabbed his leg with both hands and tried to move his foot but it was stuck firmly, as if he'd stepped in cement.

"Gustav," he shouted. "Do something!"

His teacher didn't respond. He seemed oblivious, lost in a trance.

Bedrik shook his head. "He can't hear you, Danny. He won't be able to for another thirty seconds or so. It's a very old spell, one I have no defense against. However, I don't intend to let him finish it."

"Let me go!"

"Oh, I can't do that Danny. I wish I could because I genuinely like you, but I have things to do and you're the solution I've been looking for."

"What do you mean?" His heart was racing; his eyes frightened.

"I can control this town on my own. But to expand my boundaries, I'll need more power. I'm going to take it from you." He made a slapping motion in the air, as if striking the boy. Danny's feet finally left the ground as he was knocked backward.

The man standing over his mother laughed. Danny wondered again who he was. Another possessed person, like Matt? An empty shell inhabited by a dead person? He didn't know, but that didn't stop him from hating the stranger, too. Danny stood up, but once again his feet were paralyzed.

"Do you like being helpless, Danny?" Bedrik snarled. "Of course you don't. No one does. That's what all the markings are about, you know. I've seen what you're capable of and I couldn't take any risks. But enough of this. Your mentor is almost finished; just one more stanza to go. I can't allow that."

He raised his hands to the sky, palms upward, fingers splayed, and called to the dead. All around them, the shadows moved. The shades came forth, drawn by his summons. The darkness in the cemetery solidified as the shades broke free of their graves and rose through the earth and into the sky. The shadows floated for a second and then soared toward them, screaming.

"Don't cry, Danny," Bedrik said. "Your father is here, too, and he can't wait to be reunited with you."

A shadow rose from his father's grave. Danny's eyes widened.

"Mr. Bedrik," Danny screamed. "I'm gonna kill you!"

His teacher laughed as if the threat was the funniest thing he'd ever heard. "Oh, Danny, you're a prize. All of that power and emotion just waiting to be used. I will drink you like a glass of water."

Gustav's eyes snapped open, flashing in the darkness.

"You'll do no such thing."

"Finished with your spell, old man? It won't help you. It takes time for the charge to build, and you do not have time. You won't breach the circle. The dead are coming. In a minute, you'll belong to me, as will the boy."

"No, he will not."

The shades raced towards them. The night grew blacker. The shadows' density muted the light from the fireflies. A dark shape hovered over Danny.

Son...

Danny gasped. "Dad? Daddy?"

Son...the pain...I can't...

"Danny," Gustav shouted. "The salt. Use it."

The shadow reached out with one hand and tried to force his mouth open. Still unable to move his feet, Danny clawed at it with his hands. His fingers slipped through the darkness. The shade was cold.

"Dad," he cried out. "Please..."

I'm sorry...son...let me in...

Danny shoved his hand into his pocket and pulled out the salt shaker. She sprinkled some on his father's shade, and the shadow immediately recoiled.

"Bedrik," Gustav shouted, "leave him."

"You are fond of Danny," Bedrik gloated. "You see yourself as some type of surrogate father to him, don't you? That's your weakness, Gustav, and that's why I lured the boy here. You were so eager to confront me that you never stopped to consider why I'd want your apprentice here, too. So listen up and listen well. Stand down and accept your fate. Allow yourself to be taken over. If you don't, I'll kill the boy and his mother, as well. And you know that will be just the beginning of their sufferings."

The first group of shades reached Gustav and swirled around him. Blue energy flared across his body. The shades fell back. So did Danny's father.

Gustav grinned. "I did not care why you wanted boy here. I wanted him here, too."

Bedrik frowned. "What are you talking about?"

"Boy is not my apprentice. Is not even magic. He is just my battery."

Both Danny and Bedrik stared at him. They both said it at the same time.

"What?"

Gustav's smile grew wider. He pointed one hand at Bedrik and the other at Danny. Then, sucking in a breath, he uttered a single word. Power flowed from Danny like water from a spigot, crackling in the air as it rushed from his body and into Gustav's. Danny felt drained. Empty. The surge lanced through the shades and they dissipated, fading away to nothing.

The bolt leaped through the graveyard, zipping from shadow to shadow. It burst through Danny's father.

Danny...I love...

Danny watched in horror as his father faded away.

With the shades outside the circle defeated, Gustav focused on Bedrik. The power slammed into the invisible barrier. The opposing energies flared, bathing the cemetery with a bright, white light. Danny closed his eyes and saw spots. When he opened them again, a solid stream rocketed from Gustav's outstretched hand and ripped Bedrik's shield apart, breaching the circle of protection.

Quickly, Bedrik fell to his knees and uttered a quick spell. The energy flowed over him but did not harm the teacher. Instead, it raced throughout the rest of the circle, disintegrating the shades inside the barrier. Edward T. Rammel didn't even have time to scream as he was torn from the body of Tony Amiratti Junior. Danny's mother writhed on the stone slab, untouched by the light.

Danny felt the last of his power drain away. The flow of light sputtered and then stopped. Gustav dropped his arms, panting.

"You son of a bitch," Danny muttered. "You were just using me all this time? You're just like every other adult in my life."

Gustav did not reply. His expression was grim.

Bedrik stood up slowly and brushed the dirt from his pants. "Is that the best you have, old man? You've breached my circle, destroyed my shades, but I'm still standing."

"Not for long."

Bedrik laughed. "Oh, Gustav, come on. You've no power left. You've drained both yourself and the boy. You can't possibly win. Stand down."

Gustav wiped sweat from his brow. "Danny was not just a battery. He is also an anchor."

Bedrik's smile vanished.

"Edward," he hollered. "Kill the bitch!"

"No!" Danny struggled against his invisible bonds.

The man standing next to his mother picked up an onyx knife and lowered it to her throat.

"You are too late, Bedrik," Gustav warned. "This is your end."

Behind Gustav, the night surged forward, a massive, obsidian sheet that blocked out the tombstones, the trees, even the sky. The darkness had a human face—Martin Bedrik's. Danny felt a familiar fear. This was what he'd encountered the night he'd left Gustav's, and at his home. He heard the sounds again, coming from everywhere and nowhere at once. This time, they were much louder, and when the darkness spoke, it was like thunder.

MICHAEL...

"Oh shit." Bedrik scrambled backward.

"You wanted family reunion, yes?" Gustav stood unmoving as the darkness flowed around him and raced towards the other magician. "Your brother found Danny. He has been anchored to him ever since. Following him around like a lost puppy. Not always able to breach the gulf, but tonight, I give him help. Get enough power from the boy to bring your brother through."

MICHAEL...YOU LEFT ME THERE...SO COLD...WHY...

"Martin," Bedrik stammered, "you have to understand. You have to—"

YOU ARE THE BAD TWIN, MICHAEL...

Without another word, Bedrik turned and ran. The darkness raced after him, enveloping him like a shroud. Bedrik shrieked. His face reddened as the black energies wrapped around him. He staggered backwards, trying to pull it off, but the shade seethed and swarmed, coalescing into a maelstrom of shadow intent on only one thing—revenge.

Danny watched in horror, and realized that Gustav was laughing.

Michael Bedrik screamed again as the darkness smothered him. A mouth formed of shadow and lashed out, biting deep into his body and ripping away the flesh. It bit down again and again, devouring him with an insatiable lust, a gluttonous spirit incapable of mercy and vengeful to the last. Bedrik looked at Danny, his eyes begging for help. A moment later, the blackness feasted on his eyes, too.

Danny closed his own eyes, trying to block the images. He couldn't stop the chewing sounds.

When he opened them again, there was nothing left of Mr. Bedrik, not even his clothes. The swirling black mass shifted again and again, finished with its feast. Danny felt its rage, a cold and bitter furnace of energies.

Gustav stepped forward. "Now you go back to where you came from."

THE PRISON...

"Nyet. Death is not a prison. You are free. Go to the next place and return here no more."

Gustav banished Martin Bedrik's spirit and the shadow vanished. Silence returned to the cemetery. The lightning bugs fell to the ground, dead. Darkness, normal darkness, closed in on them again. Danny took a hesitant step and found that he could move. He ran to his mother and untied her. She was unconscious.

"Will she be okay?"

"Da. She will wake up soon. You should get her home."

Danny glanced around the battleground. The man with the knife lay at the foot of the crypt.

"Gustav, what just happened here? What was that thing?"

"Martin Bedrik's spirit has been following you," Gustav said. "You found each other, yes? It latched on to you. Tried to use your power to come back and get revenge. But it did not know how and neither did you. I helped it tonight. I knew we would need him to help defeat his brother."

"You used him," Danny muttered, "just like you used me."

"Danny—"

"Don't say another fucking word. I heard what you told Mr. Bedrik. I thought you were my friend. I believed in you. You lied to me. Gave me those presents. Told me I was magic. But I'm not, am I? All this time, all you wanted was my power. You used me. Wanted what I could give you. You're just like everyone else. Just like Mom stealing my money. I hate you."

Gustav nodded sadly.

"I wish I'd never met you. Wish I'd never found that stupid body. Wish none of this had ever happened."

Gustav spoke softly. "You wish to forget?"

"What do you think, you commie asshole? Of course I do. Matt. My Dad…"

Before Danny could react, Gustav reached out and touched his forehead.

"Sleep."

Danny slumped over, as unconscious as his mother. Gustav caught him as he fell.

"You will fall again, Danny, and the next time, I will not be able to catch you." His voice choked with emotion. "I wish that I could, but I cannot. Even I am not that powerful, yes? If I could, I would fix it. I would move Hook Mountain for you. You are like son to me. But this will not happen."

He loaded the boy and his mother into the police car and drove them home. They did not wake as he tucked them into their beds. He collected the presents he'd given to Danny from the boy's room, and sobbed when he flipped through Danny's Book of Shadows.

After regaining his composure, Gustav removed all traces of himself from the house. Tomorrow, Danny and his mother would wake up with no memories of what had happened. Bedrik's death—as well as the deaths of Matt, Amiratti, and many others—would become just another statistic, the violent cost of living in Brackard's Point. In time, Danny would mend his friendship with Chuck, Ronnie, and Jeremy—whose secret name was Jammer. Gustav knew this, even if the boy did not. They would become friends again, better than ever. Danny's mother would not drink. She would get a better job and pay attention to her son. None of them would remember any of what had happened. Danny would forget all about magic.

And Danny would be happy for the rest of his brief life.

Gustav returned to the police car and drove into the night. He was tired, but there was still much to do before he went to sleep. He had to take care of the car once and for all. Tomorrow, he would begin hunting down the rest of the renegade shades, the ones Bedrik had placed inside the local government, fire and police departments, churches, and elsewhere. With their master destroyed, the shades were free to act on their own, living the lives they'd stolen. He couldn't allow the charade to continue. The dead should stay dead.

More people would vanish under mysterious circumstances over the coming days. Then, when he was finished, Brackard's Point would return to normal—whatever that may be.

He turned on the radio. Music filled the car, and Gustav sang along, his voice full of pain and regret.

"If you could read my mind, what a tale my thoughts would tell..."

Tears slid down his whiskered face.

He'd lied to the boy. Danny was indeed magic. He had the gift. The ability. Magic was a part of Danny and in time, he'd have learned it all over again, with or without Gustav's help. But Danny would not have that time. The old man's heart broke. He wept as he drove, and the heavens cried along with him.

Magic had a price.

Magic was knowledge and power and sometimes sacrifice.

182

Gustav had knowledge of Danny's fate.
He did not have the power to stop it.
And that was the heaviest sacrifice of all.

ABOUT THE AUTHORS

GEOFF COOPER was born in accordance with the prophecy. When this lamentable day transpired is unclear. The current hypothesis places the event sometime between the rise of the Babylon and the fall of Kabul. Coop's short stories have appeared in many anthologies and a magazine or two. Cemetery Dance publications published his novella, *Retribution, Inc.* He has been a mechanic, a security guard, a firefighter, a firearms instructor, a driver of cars of questionable legality, and a provider of things for those with more money than sense. Currently, he holds the title of Duck. Yeah, as in 'quack'. Don't ask: it's beyond your comprehension. He's got more opinions than the Bible has begats. Whisky tango foxtrot, over…

BRIAN KEENE lives in the backwoods of Pennsylvania, and writes books for a living. Trust us; it's not nearly as glamorous as it sounds. Just like magic, there's always a price. His previous titles include *Ghoul*, *Dead Sea*, *The Rising*, *City of the Dead*, *The Conqueror Worms*, *Fear of Gravity*, *Terminal*, and many more. Several of his books and stories have been adapted for comics, and several more are slated for film and video games. He probably owes you an email or a phone call, and promises to get around to it one of these days. He would like to take this moment to stop being a smart-ass and sincerely thank you for your patience. Visit him online at www.briankeene.com

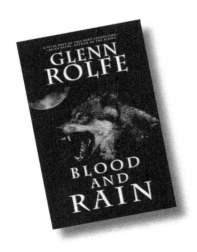

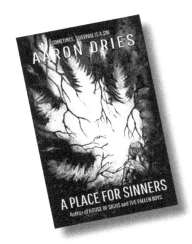

CPSIA information can be obtained
at www.ICGtesting.com
Printed in the USA
BVHW030415170220
572374BV00002B/15

9 781913 138240